RIP TYDE

H.E. GOODHUE

Severed Press
Hobart Tasmania

RIP TYDE

"Fishes live in the sea, as men do a-land; the great ones eat up the little ones."

~ William Shakespeare

-1-

This is going to save our marriage. It will give us time to sort through the pieces of a broken life and fit some of them back together. It's just like a puzzle. I used to be really good at those. The pieces will fit back together. All we need is the time to do it.

Tyde Gregory tried to calm his nerves with that bittersweet mantra as he threw the last of his things into his yellow duffle bag and zipped it closed. The nametag hung from a loop on the bottom of the bag. Tyde flipped the tag and examined his own name. Over the years, he had come to accept the fact that his parents were California surf hippies and had the best of intentions when they named him, but he would be lying if there weren't times that he really wished his nametag said 'Bob' or 'Scott' instead. Then again, his parents must have been onto to something when they named him Tyde; sure they were definitely *on* something when they did, but he couldn't deny that they seemed to instinctually know he would love the water.

Being in the water was one of the few times that Tyde ever felt truly at peace. The water brought him Wendy. Memories of her walking into his diving class all those years ago flashed through his mind. She was beautiful, tanned and giggling with her friends as they waited for the class to start. It had been one of those classes people took on vacation, half-drunk, bobbing around in the hotel pool and breathing through the regulator. No one ever really learned how to dive, but Wendy cornered Tyde after the class and insisted that he give her a private lesson. There was no way in hell Tyde was going to turn down a bikini-clad request for a private class. Wendy left after her week was up and Tyde followed. They had been inseparable since.

Life had been easy, like they were destined to be together. Wendy took a job teaching kindergarten and Tyde started working in a local dive shop. Even though he wore surf shorts to work on most days, it felt a little too corporate for him. But he was willing to deal with timesheets and inventory if it meant he got to go home to Wendy every night.

Weekends had been devoted to dive trips with friends. Everything fit together and worked. They had been happy. Their friends had been happy. The water brought them all together and made their happiness possible. Life made sense when they were diving or at least it used to.

Tyde shook his head, trying to banish thoughts of the past from his head and laughed when the mirror on top of Wendy's dresser reflected an image of the dirty blond rat's nest that blossomed from the side of his head. He didn't want to waste time getting lost in the past. He was looking towards the future. That's why they were going on this trip, or maybe it was more accurate to say that was why he was going on the trip. Wendy refused at first. Later just protested. And finally reluctantly agreed to go.

Wendy's things were already packed. She was always more prepared than Tyde, though neither of them had been prepared for last year's diving trip. No checklist or equipment double-check could have prepared them. More past that Tyde didn't want to think about. He grabbed Wendy's bag and walked towards the door. The rest of their gear was in the garage. Wendy was out there double-checking everything before the taxi came to bring them to the airport.

Tyde tried to convince himself that last year's trip was when his marriage began to fall apart, that the trauma of the trip drove a wedge between him and Wendy, but he knew that wasn't true. Things were bad before the trip, probably for longer than Tyde even knew, and the trip only made them worse.

It was true that Wendy agreed to go on this trip. That had to count for something. It had to mean there was some small splinter of hope and love left in her heart. Tyde hoped for all of those things, but knew that his wife's motivation might have more to do with the fact that they were flying to Long Island in the Bahamas to dive a blue hole. They had swam just about anywhere there was water, but never had the opportunity to explore the amazing underwater cave systems known as blue holes. Aside from Belize, the one on Long Island was probably the best in the world. This breathtaking blue world plunged over six hundred feet below sea level, opening into a honeycomb of rooms that had only just begun to be explored. It was unlike anything Tyde or Wendy had ever seen, completely alien and intoxicating.

Still, Wendy agreed to go. They weren't going to spend the entire time underwater. There would be time to talk, to reconnect. Time to save their marriage.

This is going to save our marriage. It will give us time to sort through the pieces of a broken life and fit some of them back together. It's just like a puzzle. I used to be really good at those. The pieces will fit back together. All we need is the time to do it.

Tyde repeated his mantra as Wendy greeted him with a sad, broken smile from the waiting taxi. Tyde threw the rest of their gear into the trunk of the taxi and climbed inside. He reached over and gently squeezed Wendy's hand. She looked out the window. Tyde squeezed once more, a simple, pleading gesture that spoke volumes about their relationship. Wendy's fingers fluttered in Tyde's and tightened ever so slightly.

This would work. It had to work. Tyde could fix this. He could find a way to fit these pieces together, just like all of those puzzles from so long ago. Tyde loved puzzles when he was a child. He just never wanted his marriage to become one.

-2-

The needle on Milo's air gauge ticked slightly over from yellow to red. There was plenty of air left in the tanks considering that the surface was only twenty to thirty feet overhead, but his tanks had been problematic ever since Jefferson dropped them on the dock. There had to be a small leak somewhere in the system, not that Milo and Jefferson had the money to fix it. He would need to head for the surface.

Milo signaled the three college boys he was guiding today – time to head to the surface. One of the kids held up five fingers. What harm could five more minutes do? Milo gave him the thumbs up, the college boys were experienced divers, and began swimming for the surface. He turned to watch the three college boys swimming near the wreck they had explored today. One ducked inside the ship. Experienced, not smart.

"Damn it," Milo cursed inside his head. Five minutes meant five minutes outside of the damn ship. The last thing he and Jefferson needed was one of those morons getting hurt. Milo's gauge ticked a little further into red. *"Shit,"* Milo thought. He would have to switch his tank out with one of the extras on the boat. Running out of air with only those three idiots to rely on was out of the question. Hopefully, those kids would watch the time and be close behind.

"Milo, where the hell are they?" Jefferson paced anxiously in the rear of the boat. He kept peering over the side, willing the three missing divers to break the water's glassy surface.

Treading water, Milo pulled the regulator from his mouth and pushed his mask back on his head. His thin dreadlocks glistened with the dying rays of a setting sun. Jefferson was a pain in the ass and prone to panic, but it looked like he was right. Those college kids weren't on the boat and it didn't look like they had broken the surface yet either.

"Do you see them floating anywhere nearby?" Milo asked. "They were supposed to be heading for the surface right about now. Maybe the current took them?"

"If I saw them, would I be asking you where they hell they were?" Jefferson was beginning to lose it. He and Milo had dumped all of what little money they had into opening this diving business. A crappy boat and couple of dented scuba tanks later, they were in business, but all of that would be over if something happened to these college boys. "Get your mask back on and go look!"

Milo swallowed a string of curse words, pulled his mask down and cleared his regulator. He glanced at his air gauge. There wasn't much left, but there was no time to switch his tanks out if one of those college boys was trapped in the wreck.

Maybe the three morons were still underwater screwing around. Maybe not. They were over privileged little shits, but from what Milo had seen, they knew how to dive. If he thought something like this was going to happen, he never would have taken them out past the breakers. But these three didn't want to dive near the reef with all the snorkeling soccer moms. They wanted to wreck dive near the scuttled World War II German destroyer.

At the time, Milo didn't think it would be a problem. Sure, the current was stronger and there was always the possibility of a shark or two, but neither of those things appeared to worry the college boys, so Milo pushed the worry out of his head.

The smoke stacks of the German destroyer pointed towards Milo like the barrel of a gigantic gun. He couldn't help but think that the image was all too prophetic. Tourism accounted for more than half of the Bahamian economy. If he didn't find these kids, the local authorities were going to make an international example out of him.

Swimming past the smoke stacks, Milo tried to remember the last place he had seen these idiots. He checked his air gauge. Not much was left in the tanks. It had to be the same for those kids, probably less with their excited, quick breathing emptying the tank.

As the War wound down, the Germans scuttled their own ships instead of surrendering to the allies. The Nazis would set a charge in the powder room and jump ship. A handful of these destroyers were scattered around the islands, having turned into artificial reefs over the years and become tourist attractions.

A large hole, ringed in jagged metal teeth loomed in the side of the ship. Milo envisioned the explosion that created this hole and remembered seeing one of the kids swimming towards it. He thought that one might have been named Chet or Chad or something along those lines. It was Chad. Milo remembered thinking it was one of the worst names he had ever heard, though he had to admit it kind of fit the kid. A few more kicks propelled Milo down to the gaping hole.

The setting sun and depth made it difficult to see. A large, handheld spotlight hung from Milo's harness. He reached back and clicked it on. A yellowed beam of light cut through the darkness inside the ruined ship. Motes of algae, ragged bits of seaweed and other unidentifiable detritus drifted lazily inside of the hull. Milo panned the light from side to side.

The corner of a large blue and white flipper peered out from around the corner of what looked to have once been a set of stairs. Milo watched the flipper move gently. He hoped it was Chad or one of the others and that they had just lost track of time while exploring. Milo swam towards the flipper. He wished that he could have called out to the kid, just told him to stop screwing around and get his ass back to the boat.

The flipper peeked out a little more. Milo kicked hard, throwing clouds of underwater refuse swirling around his head. With his free hand, Milo grabbed the flipper and yanked. He figured it might startle the little turd, maybe send images of a shark swimming through his head – it was the least Milo could do to repay the favor.

A torn stump of flesh jutted from the flipper in Milo's hand. Raw, red strips of flesh and meat danced in the light current, surrounding a white, splintered shank of bone. A muffled cry erupted in a cloud of bubbles as Milo gnashed his teeth into the length of rubber in his mouth. Bile burned Milo's throat. He wanted to vomit, wanted to scream. He needed to keep his regulator in place.

Pushing away from the leg, Milo swam for the hole in the side of the destroyer. Thoughts of what could have done this flooded his mind and panic twisted around his heart. What if it was still in the ship's hull? What if it was behind him?

Milo couldn't stand not knowing. He turned and shone his light behind him, half expecting to see a gaping maw of white, pointed teeth. There was nothing, only the errant clouds of…of meat.

The water was teeming with torn hunks of shredded flesh. A severed finger, trailing ribbons of tattered skin like the tentacles of some hellish jellyfish gently bumped Milo's mask. Milo swallowed hard. He was no longer able to fight the urge to vomit. It surged up his throat and, with no other exit available, gushed out Milo's nostrils, filling the lower half of his mask. The acidic tang of puke stung his eyes and made it difficult to see. Milo wanted to dump his mask, but feared letting in the revolting stew of seawater and human meat. With no other option, Milo turned and swam for the surface, not caring that a gurgled scream knocked his regulator free from his mouth.

The regulator bumped against Milo's side as he swam for the surface. He could have cleared it and returned his air flow, but he didn't want to stop and risk finding out what had done that to Chad.

"Where are they?" Jefferson almost shrieked when he saw Milo break the surface alone.

Milo ignored his friend's question and swam for the platform on the back of the boat.

"Where are they?" Jefferson repeated.

"Get me in the boat!" Milo cried as he pulled himself onto the platform. "Get the tanks off of me. Get me out of the water."

"What happened down there? Where are they? Why won't you answer me?" Jefferson couldn't stop the stream of questions as he helped Milo out of his harness and dropped the air tanks onto the deck of the boat. "What is that crap stuck in your hair?" Jefferson plucked a ragged, pink chunk from Milo's hair. He examined it, trying to determine its origin. "Is this chum or something?"

"It's Chad," Milo gagged. Vomit splattered across the deck of the boat.

"Chad?" Jefferson dropped the bit of meat as if it had suddenly become hot and leapt back. "What could do that to Chad?"

"The Lusca," Milo gagged between dry heaves.

Jefferson was done asking questions. He turned to rush towards the steering wheel, but slipped in Milo's vomit and belly flopped onto the deck.

Milo stepped over his friend, who floundered in an acrid puddle of puke, and started the engines. The dual Mercury outboards roared to life and almost lifted the boat out of the water before rocketing it across the water.

-3-

"There are caves all throughout the world's bodies of water," Dr. Lenny Borges snapped. "Why is it so hard to believe that some of these caves would be connected?"

Lenny detested wasting time arguing with military brass. They were only concerned with one thing – results. Science was not only about results. It was a labor of love and investigation. His research was akin to writing a beautiful concerto. It simply could not be done in a day, not that the people gathered before him had even the slightest inkling about the devotion and love his research required. No, these were the kind of men would preferred the jaunty tune of a kazoo to the melodic wanderings and wonderment found in a classical piece. But they were also the kind of men who signed his checks and kept his research funded, so Lenny was willing to suffer their ignorance a little longer.

"So what?" one of the generals shrugged. "Who gives a one wet fart about a series of underwater caves?"

"You should," Lenny grinned. "These caves run miles below sea level, well beyond the accepted boundaries of any nation on the map. What we have here is a virtual subway system that could take supplies, soldiers or even bombs, anywhere on the globe completely undetected." They were silent. That was good. He had their attention. "Gentlemen, there are known, and soon to be known, blue holes located throughout the world. If you're not interested, I'm sure someone else will be."

"Enough with the hollow threats," another said. "Continue."

A map of the Earth was projected on the screen behind them. Lenny clicked a button on his laptop and what looked like the inside of an anthill appeared over the map. "These are the known caves that connect. Many of these have only recently begun to be explored. Civilian grade diving equipment simply does not allow for extended exploration of these systems, but with the new technology developed in my labs, we will be able to traverse these systems and ultimately turn them into a transportation and delivery system for whatever makes you smile."

"What about that one there?" one of the men seated at the table asked. He pointed at the marker for a large cave that had recently been discovered near a small island off the East Coast of the United States. Lenny knew he had once been told their names, but he had never cared enough to remember them. The wrinkles and folds of his brain were reserved for information that actually mattered.

"What about it?" Lenny demanded. "It is no different from any of the others, perhaps only slightly warranting more attention because it was recently discovered."

"That's Sunset Island, if I'm not mistaken," the man continued. "Wasn't there recently an...*incident* there? Are there risks of another such *incident*?"

"I believe what occurred on Sunset Island was unique, but if I'm not mistaken," Lenny paused, "you recently authorized the reopening of a government facility on the neighboring Peach Island. Don't you think my research could benefit those endeavors? You can't possibly deny that our government isn't just the slightest bit interested in knowing what's down there and how we could benefit from it. Besides, our government has known about these types of *incidents* for decades, so let's not waste time pretending otherwise."

"We have never acknowledged the existence of the creature that woke near Sunset Island," one of the men said, but his voice lacked conviction. Lenny's accusation had put him into press conference mode.

Lenny laughed. "The Loch Ness Monster? The Ogopogo? The Lusca? Megalodon? All of these creatures have been labeled as folklore and fantasy, but everyone in this room knows the truth, gentlemen. These creatures exist and if we are going to take advantage of what I have proposed, then we need to understand the ecosystem that exists within these tunnels."

"Fine," one of the generals grunted. "Let's say your aquatic boogeymen are real, so what? What does that have to do with your research? We don't need to understand what we can easily kill. For God's sake, they killed the Sunset Island monster with a fuel truck and a damn ferry. I think we've got capabilities that extend a little beyond that."

Lenny sighed. What little patience he had for these men was gone. "Whether or not people realize it, the tunnels running between blue holes can be traced to every major body of water where these creatures are sighted."

"And?" someone snapped.

"And all it will take to collapse them and completely ruin what I have proposed is one thick headed moron sending a bomb down there to deal with one of my *aquatic boogeymen*. I would much rather increase our nation's military strength instead of blowing up a tunnel and forcing all of these creatures, who's existence we evidently don't acknowledge, out into open water creating an endless string of Sunset Island incidents."

A wave of hushed conversations and mummers passed through the room. Lenny waited. He already knew the answer.

"We will authorize your research," one of the men nodded. "Where is the first site you plan on investigating?"

"I have selected a site in the Bahamas," Lenny pointed a red dot on the map.

"Aren't you worried about the level of tourist traffic that passes through there?" one of the men asked.

"Quite the contrary, that is exactly why I selected this site," Lenny answered. "If I were to go to one of the more remote or obscure sites, we would attract attention. My crew and I will blend in and no one will be any the wiser. We will just be another group of sun-hungry tourists. There isn't the slightest thing to worry about."

"For your sake, we certainly hope so, Dr. Borges." The shadowy gathering of men closed their folders and stood in unison before shuffling out of the room.

Lenny paid no attention to their idle threat. It was all part of the game. They needed to appear to be in control. But a playground peeing contest was of no concern to Lenny. He had his funding – any other problems could be dealt with once he arrived in the Bahamas.

-4-

The plane ride to the Bahamas was blessedly short. Tyde tried and failed multiple times to strike up a conversation with Wendy, but she either pretended to be sleeping or interested in the grainy movie playing on the screen in the headrest in front of her. It looked like another one of those straight to video shit shows that always seemed to find their way on to an airplane.

"How does Nicholas Cage keep making movies?" Tyde smirked as he elbowed Wendy's arm. She cast a sideways glance and half-hearted smile. "There has to be some bet those Hollywood ding dongs keep losing. Or maybe they play Truth or Cage?"

"Yeah, maybe," Wendy nodded and returned to watching the cinematic travesty displayed before her.

There had been a time when Tyde's sense of humor would have Wendy howling, laughing so hard that people would stop and look. Tyde missed that laugh. He missed Wendy.

It was odd how someone could still be there, could still sleep next to you every night, but be completely gone. It was like Wendy had shed her skin and that was all that was left for Tyde. Just a shell. And right now that shell was choosing Nick Cage over her husband of seven years. It wasn't the first time Tyde felt like he was losing Wendy to someone else. It was just the first time that the guy was four inches tall and two-dimensional.

"Hey, look." Tyde leaned across Wendy's lap and pointed out the small window. A brilliant blue sea spread beneath the plane and shone like a sapphire in Neptune's crown. "It's beautiful."

Wendy looked out the window and a real smile, the first Tyde had seen in a long time, curled the edges of her lips. "It is beautiful," she agreed.

"You're beautiful," Tyde added before he could stop the cheesy words from spilling out of his mouth. But it was true. Seeing Wendy smile was beautiful. He didn't care how trite it sounded – he meant every word.

Tyde reached for Wendy's hand.

"Yeah, thanks," Wendy answered and pulled her hand away from Tyde's to push her headphones back in place.

"Do you want another drink?" the steward asked as he looked at the empty plastic cup on Tyde's tray.

"Sure," Tyde nodded, thankful for the distraction. "Could I please get another beer?"

"No problem," the steward nodded and retrieved the can from the drink cart. "I don't know how he does it," he said, passing the can to Tyde.

"Excuse me?" Tyde asked, taking the can.

"Nicholas Cage," the steward clarified. "I don't know how he keeps getting work. It's like someone lost a bet."

"Yeah," Tyde nodded, glancing at Wendy. "Someone is definitely losing."

The problem was that it was Tyde.

-5-

"What do you mean it was the Lusca?" someone shouted from the crowd that gathered on the dock. "Everyone knows the Lusca isn't real. That's just some bunk fairytale."

Milo could barely contain his anger. Sure, everyone knew the Lusca was a fairytale, everyone who moved to the island from somewhere else. Anyone who had half a brain and even a drop of true Bahamian blood knew the Lusca was real.

"So a giant octopus ate those kids?" someone else asked sarcastically.

"You didn't see what Milo saw," Jefferson protested. Milo noticed that he still stood in the boat. Maybe he was scared to get onto the dock or maybe it was so he could make a quick getaway. Either would have been a reasonable explanation. But Milo wasn't about to take responsibility for something he didn't do.

"Look, I didn't see the Lusca, I'll give you that, but you tell me what else could do that to those kids?" Milo pulled his gear up from the boat. He also wasn't going to waste time sitting around on the docks arguing with drunks and tourists.

"Where do you think you're going?" someone shouted.

"I'm not going to stand around here playing grab ass with a dock full of morons." Milo marched towards the crowd. "Now unless you're going to call the RBDF, then get the hell out of my way."

Milo pushed a little deeper into the crowd before he ran into a wall of blue shirts and navy pants. A series of black berets dotted the heads set along the wall. Evidently, someone had called the Royal Bahamas Defense Force. With no real need for a huge military or police force, the RBDF was somewhat of a catch all, handling everything from patrolling the waters to working as local law enforcement to maintain order. Three tourists going missing, and possibly being eaten, would definitely fall under the broad umbrella of the RBDF's duties.

Milo groaned as one of the largest officers broke rank with the others and addressed the crowd.

"We need everyone to vacate this area," the officer bellowed. A small machine gun hung from a strap on his right shoulder. Milo seemed to recall being told that it was an H&K MP5, but wouldn't have put money on it. The only kind of gun he felt comfortable with was a spear gun. "Unless you have information that may assist with locating these missing divers, we need you to leave immediately. Thank you for your cooperation."

At the end of the officer's final sentence, the other men sprang to life and began ushering people off the dock.

"Hi Milo," the officer nodded.

"Officer Banks," Milo said like it tasted foul.

"Come on, Milo," Officer Banks winced. "You know all that officer crap isn't necessary. Just call me Stan."

"Stan?" Milo laughed. "Why not His Royal Highness, the Prince of Poopy Pants, like I used to?" "Because we're not six anymore," Stan grinned. "And besides, it really pisses Mom off when you call me that. Besides, I have a gun." He patted the machine gun that hung from his shoulder.

Milo shrugged. "Stan it is then." Milo and his twin brother had never seen eye to eye. The fact that Stan was almost a good foot taller certainly didn't help, but it went far deeper than that. A bitter divorce had divided the brothers, each loyal to a different parent. After their father died, they found a way to tolerate one another, but Milo never felt comfortable around his mother or twin brother. They were too much alike and he was far too different. If he was honest, there were days that Milo doubted they were even related.

Their parents told Milo and Stand that they were twins, and for the most part they accepted it as fact, but the two brothers could not have looked any more different. Stan was a wall of straight-laced muscle that was chomping at the bit to enlist in the RBDF and quickly became a ranking officer. Milo, on the other hand, barely finished school and started a diving business with Jefferson, largely because it allowed him to set his own hours and didn't require doing something he wouldn't already have been doing.

"Mom wants to know if you're coming over for dinner tonight," Stan continued. "She said you never returned her call." Milo thought it was amazing that even with everything going on, Stan still found time to be a momma's boy.

"Shouldn't you be more worried about the fact that the fucking Lusca just ate three tourists?" Milo almost shouted.

"Stop yelling all that foolishness and getting the tourists worried." Stan finally looked angry. "The last thing we need is your dumb ass turning this tragedy into an economic disaster."

"Then you tell me Wonder Twin, what the hell did that to those kids?" Milo demeaned. "What could shred three grown men in under five minutes? One minute they were there – next minute chum. Sure sounds like the Lusca to me."

"That's enough," Stan growled and removed his handcuffs from their leather holster.

"You're arresting me?" Milo took a step towards his brother. "For what? Don't you have more important things to go do?"

"I'm not arresting you," Stan said as spun Milo around and cinched the cuffs around his wrists. "The RBDF is already out patrolling the wreck and dive site. If anything comes up, they'll radio me. What I'm doing is protecting you from yourself…and I'm taking you to Mom's for dinner."

"To dinner? In handcuffs?" Milo strained against handcuffs. "What about Jefferson?"

"Jefferson?" Stan shouted. "You hungry?"

Jefferson looked at the cold vomit caked on the front of his shorts and t-shirt. It had begun to harden in the cool salty breeze that rolled in with the waves.

"I could eat," Jefferson shrugged. "But I'm not wearing handcuffs." He climbed out of the boat and onto the dock. The wind changed direction and blew towards Stan and Milo.

"You're not wearing those clothes either," Stan motioned towards the puke-laden outfit. "Go change. You smell disgusting."

-6-

Flying to the Bahamas in the back of a government freighter was not exactly Lenny's idea of a good time, but there was no way his equipment and crew would have gone unnoticed on a commercial flight. Once the plane touched down, Lenny watched his team load the large yellow plastic crates into the backs of four passenger vans. With a thriving tourist industry, the island had plenty of these vans and Lenny felt they would easily blend in.

The vans rolled into Clarence Town, the capital of Long Island. It was a cute town with about 350 residents, a grocery store, pub and a few other shops, but not much else. Lenny turned his attention to one of the two docks located in Clarence Town. A mail boat unloaded bundles of letters and packages from the other islands.

"Must be the government dock," Lenny muttered to no one in particular. A few of his research assistants turned to look, but knew better than to answer. They would know if Lenny was talking to them.

Having been an employee of the US Government, Lenny was amazed at the lax security of the RBDF dock. A few officers milled around the dock and buildings, but none appeared to have the high strung intensity or purpose that Lenny observed in the soldiers assigned to protect his research. Four of these men were in plain clothes, disguised as research assistants, but cargo shorts or not, Lenny thought they were pretty easily identified as soldiers.

"Dr. Borges," Cal Rodgers said from the driver's seat of the van. Cal was Lenny's longest standing assistant, which lead a few of the newer ones to guess he was also the favorite, but time had done little to endear one to the other.

"What is it, Cal?" Lenny asked. Cal had the annoying habit of pointing out problems, instead of fixing them.

Cal brought the van to a slow stop and pointed through the windshield. The three vans following behind rolled up close behind.

Lenny followed the direction of Cal's finger to where two men were arguing in the middle of the street.

"Drive around them," Lenny barked.

"Can't." Cal pointed towards a knot of people that slowly drifted from the dock and into the street to watch the altercation. They must have followed the men from the dock where this stupidity began.

"Then go through them." Lenny turned his attention away from the fight. Some people found these types of displays entertaining, but Lenny could not have cared less. Examining those basest elements of the human psyche that evolution had forgotten to extinguish held not even the slightest bit of interest for Lenny. He knew these things dwelled within all people – himself included, but saw no reason in publicly celebrating them.

"Dr. Borges, I can't get the van through there," Cal protested.

"I see your mouth moving Cal, but not the van," Lenny grunted. "Should I entertain even the slightest hope in seeing the opposite at some point today?"

"I can't drive over people," Cal continued.

"No," Lenny shook his head. "You won't. There is a difference."

"You know you're probably the biggest asshole I've ever met," Cal smiled without an ounce of humor.

"From you, I'll take that as a compliment," Lenny answered without looking. "Besides, it's not like they wouldn't move. All I asked you to do was give them a little incentive to do it sooner, rather than later."

"Well, I'm not going to," Cal said.

"You're lucky that your services as a research assistant far exceed your less useful qualities." Lenny removed a radio from the side pocket of his short. "You're also lucky that there are people in my employ who do not suffer from similar limitations."

Lenny barked an order into the radio and four men slipped out of the third van. They walked towards the crowd, slipped through the onlookers and approached the two men fighting. The men paused, as if surprised to see these four tourists walking into the middle of their altercation. Within a matter of seconds, the four plain-clothes soldiers split into two equal groups and dropped both fighters to the ground.

"See," Lenny smiled, rife with satisfaction.

"I see that your solution just made a bigger problem," Cal chortled.

A large RBDF officer, flanked by two civilians stood between the soldiers shouting orders. More RBDF officers threaded through the tangled mess of onlookers.

The four soldiers stood up, holding their hands out in a show of submission. Two RBDF officers pulled the original fighters up from the street and sent them walking off in opposite directions. The crowd began to thin and disperse as the soldiers, accompanied by the large RBDF officer, made their way back to the vans.

Once the soldiers were back in the van, Lenny demanded that Cal start driving, but the officer signaled for them to stop.

"What?" Lenny snapped as he rolled down his window. "What is the damn problem?"

"Problem?" the officer grinned. "I'd say that those four men assaulting the other two could be a pretty big problem. We don't stand for that kind of behavior around here."

"Oh," Lenny nodded, "I guess that would explain why those two men were beating the crap out of each other and delaying our progress in the first place."

"They were having a disagreement," the officer replied. His voice remained calm the entire conversation, but his presence and size were threat enough. "Locals have strong ideas…sometimes these ideas don't agree."

"They were fighting about a fucking fish or something." One of the soldiers angrily reported via radio from one of the other vans.

"All that over a fish?" Lenny asked with comically arched eyebrows.

"Not a fish," the officer clarified. "They were arguing about the Lusca. There was an accident earlier today and some of the more superstitious citizens believe the Lusca might be responsible. As you can see, these beliefs run pretty deep."

"I'm going to guess that's some sort of Bahamian folklore boogey man," Lenny added, feigning ignorance of the creature.

"Something like that," the officer answered as he peered into the van. The large yellow crates caught his attention.

"Stan, you and I both know the Lusca is no boogey man," a smaller man with dreadlocks chimed in from behind the officer. He was handcuffed. "The Lusca is a giant octopus and it's real."

"Milo, you and Jefferson get back to the car," the officer snapped.

"Going diving?" Milo asked, spying the crates. "Stan, those crates have diving equipment in them. With the Lusca out there, you can't let these guys go in the water."

"What kind of accident are you talking about?" Cal shouted across Lenny. "I'm not going anywhere near a giant octopus."

"A diving one," the officer said. He eyed Milo, silently demanding that he shut his mouth. "It was unfortunate, but had nothing to do with a giant octopus. It was an accident, that's all."

"You're heading through town," Milo said. "Probably heading for Dean's, aren't you?"

"The Blue Hole?" Cal asked. "Is that where the Lusca was? Is that where the accident happened?" He was clearly worried.

"No," the officer snapped and pushed Milo away from the window.

"Well, that's all the reassurance I need," Lenny nodded and began rolling up the window.

The man with dreadlocks leapt forward and grabbed the edge of the window, the handcuffs rattling on the glass. "Whatever it is you're planning, don't do it. Don't go in the water." The officer grabbed the man and pried him from the window.

"Just be careful," the officer said. He paused and looked towards the other vans. "And whatever it is you're going to do over at Dean's Blue Hole, make sure it doesn't cause any more problems for my town. If I catch you or your friends getting into any more trouble, I'll lock your asses away until the Americans make me let you out."

Lenny laughed. "I can assure you officer, that it wouldn't be too long before they did. Have a good day."

Lenny rolled the window up the rest of the way and motioned for Cal to continue driving.

-7-

"Don't go in the water until I get home from work. Don't let me catch you messing around on the rocks. Don't do this. Don't do that. Don't have fun. Blah blah blah."

Sometimes Wally Crain seriously doubted his mother's ability to start a sentence without the word 'don't.' But then again, Wally's entire life seemed to be a series of don'ts. His mother meant well, he knew that, but she worried too much and wanted to protect him by keeping him away from the world.

Wally imagined that things might be different if he had a father. His dad would take him on adventures and let him do all things the other kids in his class got to do. His dad wouldn't tell him not to go down to the beach and go snorkeling. Surely a father would understand a boy's need to test boundaries and explore. Some things a mother just didn't or couldn't understand.

But as it was, Wally didn't have a father. He never knew him and his mother always changed the subject when he tried to talk about it. Without a father, Wally figured it was up to him to push boundaries and do the stupid things that all boys were supposed to do.

Not being allowed to do much left Wally with little escape and few friends. What he did have was books. His mother never said 'don't' when it came to a book. Between the pages, Wally found the adventure and friendship his mother's overprotective nature denied him.

The stories of pirates and sea adventures were always Wally's favorite. Living on an island that had such a rich pirate-based history made the stories almost irresistible. Sunken wrecks surrounded the island, many were little more than splinters and barnacles, but they once held pirates and battled the Royal Navy on the high seas. These were the adventures Wally longed for. That was where he knew he belonged. It was also where he could never be.

Not that Wally wanted to be a pirate. Pirates these days were a totally different thing and nothing that Wally was interested in becoming. But a historian who studied the wrecks, who dove for treasure and taught others about the amazing history that had built their island, well that was something Wally longed for.

Whenever he could sneak away or if his mother worked a double shift, Wally would spend his time in the water. The mask, snorkel and fins Wally kept hidden in the garage were his ticket to a different world, a world his mother couldn't control and make boring with her rules. In the water, Wally was free to explore. He had swam near wrecked ships, come eye to eye with fish almost as big as him and he had done it all without his mother's knowledge.

A new library book gifted Wally with a map of all the known wrecks around the island. Some were too far away for Wally to get to before his mother came home, but there was one nearby, one he could get to on his bike without his mother knowing.

Stashing his bike in the bushes, Wally tossed his shirt over the handlebars and slipped the strap of his mask over his head. He blew air through the snorkel to make sure it was clear. Somewhere in the back of his mind, Wally could hear his mother's voice ragging on and on about spiders and other tiny poisonous creatures. He wished that he could shake her nagging, but some of her words had fallen like seeds between the folds of his brain and taken root. Try as he might, Wally couldn't rip the roots free.

The water was clear and beautiful – the exact opposite of Wally's mind. Wetting his feet, Wally slipped his fins on and pulled his mask into place. He leaned forward and let the gentle embrace of the next wave pull him into the serenity of the water. Fish darted, fleeing from Wally's shadow. Here he was noticed. Here the fish cared that Wally was there. He couldn't say that for most places in his life.

Wally kicked harder, rising and falling with the waves that rolled towards the sandy white beach. Sliding into the trough of the next wave, Wally's attention was pulled to a large shadow.

The outline of something massive and old waited for Wally. The masts had broken and most of the ship had collapsed, but there was no mistaking that this had once been a pirate ship. A handful of large wooden ribs jutted from the sandy bottom like the carcass of a long dead whale. To most people this was just garbage, something the ocean had yet to fully reclaim. But Wally knew better. This mangled pile of soggy wood had seen things no one could image. This ship was something amazing. It was a treasure worth more than any gold or jewels it had once carried.

The ship called to Wally, beckoned him to swim closer, to go just a little further away from the safety of the beach.

"You shouldn't be out here, Wally. Don't swim out that far. Don't go out past the waves. Don't go where it's so deep and the current is too strong."

Wally ignored his mother's words; they were easier to dismiss with his head in the water and the muffled swish of the waves echoing in his ears.

The call of the ship could not be ignored. It was all Wally could focus upon. It was why he had gotten out of bed this morning.

He kicked harder. He pushed his legs to propel him just a little closer to the ship. Something amazing waited for Wally beneath the waves.

Wally almost smiled when he thought about how wrong his mother had been. She had been so worried about him and nothing had happened. There was nothing in the water that she needed to get so worked up over.

This was where Wally belonged. This was his world.

-8-

Something was happening in the street. Tyde couldn't tell what, but a lot of people looked upset. A few vans idled near the crowd. Four guys got out of one of the vans and stomped towards the center of the knot of shouting people. They were the clothes of tourists, but moved with the uptight air of authority. These guys were probably soldiers or at the very least cops. Tyde could tell that much.

A few minutes later, the guys were marched back to the van by a large man in a RBDF officer's uniform. Tyde couldn't hear what they were saying, but it was definitely angry. The RBDF officer said something into the passenger side window of the lead van. A wiry man with thin dreads leapt towards the window only to be pulled away by the officer.

"What's going on?" Wendy asked. Tyde could tell it was more out of boredom than true interest. Wendy was never drawn in by arguments of barroom shoving matches.

"Bunch of idiots yelling about something stupid, I'm sure," Tyde shrugged.

"They're in the way," Wendy said.

"I'm sure the vans will get through," Tyde said. "Looks like the island cops are there."

"Not the vans," Wendy sighed. "They're all coming from the docks. Isn't that where we were supposed to find this guy, Martin or whatever, that you found online? We need to charter his boat, don't we?"

"Milo," Tyde corrected. "And you're right about that. It does look like they're all coming from the docks. I wonder what got them so worked up."

"Doesn't matter," Wendy said. "Looks like it's over. Let's get this over with."

Tyde stumbled one step forward and stopped.

"What is it?" Wendy asked over her shoulder.

"Why do you have to be like that? Why do we have to be like that?" Tyde asked.

"What are you talking about?" Wendy demanded.

"Talking about getting things over with, like this is the final hurrah for us," Tyde paused. "Wendy, we're on vacation to get away from all that negative shit we left at home. I didn't pack any of that in my bag and I was kind of hoping you didn't either."

"You're such a drama queen." A thin smile curled the edges of Wendy's mouth.

"Huh?" Tyde mumbled. He expected her to get angry or cold or a million other things, but getting called a drama queen was a new one.

"I meant get walking through the crowd over with you dumb ass, not get our time together over with." Wendy gave Tyde's shoulder a gentle punch and walked off towards the thinning crowd.

She smiled. Tyde couldn't keep the thought from ricocheting through his mind. It had been a small smile, but it was a smile.

This is going to save our marriage. It will give us time to sort through the pieces of a broken life and fit some of them back together. It's just like a puzzle. I used to be really good at those. The pieces will fit back together. All we need is the time to do it.

-9-

"Why'd you let those people go to Dean's?" Milo demanded. Jefferson rode in the back of Stan's police car. This was not the first time, though he had gotten in voluntarily this go round. Jefferson tried to pretend that he was not listening to the two brothers fight, but every so often he caught Stan's eyes in the rearview mirror and winced. Milo was many things – most of them the opposite of his brother, but Jefferson knew there was one thing he was not – a liar. If Milo said the Lusca killed those kids, then Jefferson was ready to accept that as the truth.

Growing up on Long Island, and never really leaving, gave Milo and Jefferson a somewhat narrow view of the world, but nothing could open up one's mind like time spent out on the open water. On their boat, they had seen things that were never visible from land. They had stared into a horizon that seemed to continue on until it dropped off the edge of the Earth. They had seen the ocean turn against men like an angry lover and knew better than to tempt her rage.

Time in the water, diving among rocks and wrecks had shown them even more. Science knew much, knew the names of many creatures that called the sea home, but that had never stopped Milo and Jefferson from spying a fish that could never be found between the pages of a book. The ocean had many secrets. The Lusca was one of them. Old timers on the island still remembered to fear the Lusca, but the young had written it off as nothing more than a drunken folk tale like the Chickcharnie.

Milo's father had taught him better. He knew that the old rules could be forgotten, but never really went away. No, the Lusca and Chickcharnie were real and Milo knew it. He had seen huge shadows beneath the waves and watched strange bird-like creatures scuttle through the pine forests of Andros. Milo knew better than to take either creature for granted. The Lusca would drag you into one of its many underwater caves and shred the meat from your bones. The Chickcharnies were little more than odd-looking, two-toed birds, but if someone was foolish enough to mock one or ignore it, they would find themselves cursed and in a living Hell. The way Milo and his father looked at it, you lost nothing by giving these creatures a little respect and healthy fear, but you could lose everything if you ignored them or wrote them off as folklore.

"I didn't let them go there, Milo," Stan finally answered. "They were going there anyway. Besides, that's not where you were this morning."

"But you didn't stop them, either," Milo argued.

"And everyone knows the Lusca lives in Blue Holes," Jefferson added.

"And here I always thought it lived in the bottle of rum bottles," Stan snorted.

"See," Milo pointed, "that kind of ignorance is what's going to get those idiots killed."

Stan's knuckles popped as he squeezed the steering wheel. He loved his brother. Sure, they were different and had never really gotten along, but that never stopped someone from loving their sibling. That was just one of nature's laws. Still, even the love of a brother had its limits and Milo was quickly approaching them. Stan had worked hard to become a respected officer of the RBDF and he was not about to have it screwed up by his brother's unlicensed diving business and insistence on the existence of a giant octopus.

"It's not real," Stan said through his teeth. "You and Dad might have thought it was and sure, Dad kind of paid his bills singing bar songs about shit like the Lusca and the Chickcharnies, but they were just stories, Milo. What happened to those kids was a terrible accident. Maybe a rouge shark or something, but it wasn't the damn Lusca and you're going to need to stop saying that it was." An unspoken threat hung on Stan's words, filling the patrol car. Jefferson shifted uncomfortably behind the cage that blocked the rear seat from the front.

"Or what?" Milo asked. "What's going to happen to me, huh? Am I going to screw up my aspiring political careers? Oh wait, no that's not me. It's you, Stan. Let's just be honest, you want me to shut up so you can continue to stick your nose a little higher up the butts of the right people."

"Honest?" Stan asked as he pulled the car on the gravel shoulder of the road. "You want honest, Milo?"

"Sure, why not?" Milo glared at his twin brother.

Stan kept his hands wrapped around the steering wheel, as if afraid of what they might do if he let go.

"The truth is, Milo, that if you don't start selling the story that this was a shark or something else that will be quickly forgotten, then people are going to keep digging in to it and more eyes will be on you. And more questions. Questions, like why didn't you have a license and what kind of punishment should you face or how badly will the families of those kids sue you? This is a total fucking shit storm, Milo, and all I'm trying to do is find some way that we all come out of it without smelling like we spent the last month sleeping in the bottom of an outhouse."

"Really?" Milo snapped. "You think that was fair? Fuck you, Stan."

"I feel like I'm missing out on something here," Jefferson said from the back of the car. "What'd I miss?"

"You mean besides every grade after sixth?" Milo asked.

"Shut up, Milo," Jefferson said as he kicked the back of the front seat.

"Don't kick the seat," Stan warned, but smiled as he turned around the face Jefferson. "I can't believe that Milo never told you about his outhouse adventure. Seems like something you two would gab about during one of your BFF slumber parties."

"Shut. Up. Stan." Milo growled.

"No, you shut up," Stan said, "or I'll taser your dumb ass and tell the story anyway."

Milo groaned, but stopped arguing.

"So, you remember that big hurricane when we were kids, probably about ten years old or so?" Stan asked. Jefferson nodded. "Well, your buddy here had to ride that bad boy out in the bottom of our father's outhouse. He ended up getting stuck down there and spent damn near two days sloshing around before someone heard him screaming and pulled him hurricane passed out on the living room floor," Stan clarified. "The entire house came out."

"Where was your dad?" Jefferson asked.

"Drunk." Milo's words were flat and factual.

"He spent the entire hurricane passed out as the house came down around him, but wouldn't you know it, the drunk bastard was fine. Same thing couldn't be same for Milo here."

"Fuck you," Milo said.

"That's really sad," Jefferson said. He leaned forward, as if to comfort his friend through the cage dividing them. "I'm sorry Milo, that's a really shitty story."

Stan's broad shoulders began to tremble and bounce as he tried to keep the laughter contained in his muscular body. Soon both Stan and Jefferson were laughing uncontrollably.

"Just fucking drive," Milo groaned.

Stan wiped a tear away from the corner of his eye and shifted the car into drive.

-10-

Wally's lungs burned as he swam towards the wreck. His body protested and demanded that he return to the surface, but Wally pushed himself further. The ship called out to him. He needed to get as close as possible. He would never touch it, but not because he would not reach it. No, it was an act of reverence. His fingers could destroy what remained of the ship and Wally refused to play any role in the destruction of this amazing piece of his island's history.

The deck of the ship had collapsed inward. The ship lay on its side, half having splintered into nothing or having been buried beneath the white sand. The mast had snapped in half and fallen to the sea floor. If someone had not known where to look, they would have easily overlooked the upper section of mast as nothing more than a rise in the sand, but Wally knew better. He knew to respect the ship and how to view it through the intelligent eyes of a historian.

Acid burned in Wally's throat. His blood beat against the sides of his head. His heart slammed against his sternum, demanding that he return to the surface and feed it oxygen. Wally turned away from the sunken ship and kicked towards the surface. The sun sparkled and danced across the water's surface like liquid fire – it was almost as beautiful as the sunken ship…almost.

A jolt shuddered through Wally's legs and sent him spiraling through a soup of bubbles and tiny panicked sea creatures. Terror flared in his chest. What hit him? Had some large school of fish or a shark just slammed into him? Wally searched the seafloor, desperate to name what just touched him. His legs ached. There would be a bruise he would have to explain away to his mother. Maybe he fell riding his bike or tripped over the coffee table. The coffee table was probably a safer choice.

Wally kicked and again headed for the surface, but paused and decided to cast one more longing glance at the ship, his ship. He was done for today, but he would return.

A dark shape detached itself from the sunken in deck of the ship. Wally opened his mouth to scream and sucked in a lungful of seawater. The salty water burned as it gushed down his throat. His mind became clouded. It felt long and drawn out, maybe even slowed down, but it had only been a matter of seconds. That was how quick life could change from vibrant and promising to over. It took some people years to die, others only seconds. Wally fought the urge to suck in another lungful of water, but lost. He was drowning.

Beneath Wally darkness opened and spread, unfurling coils of lengthy tentacles. The idea that he was blacking out flashed through his mind, but the darkness was ridged with a series of jagged white spikes. No, not spikes – teeth.

A second jolt thundered through Wally's body. He felt electricity dance up his legs and expand in his gut. He pushed thoughts of dying to the back of his head and kicked for the surface, but went nowhere. Wally kicked again. His legs stung from the impact, burned and protested as he urged them to move. Still, Wally went nowhere.

A thin tendril of red spiraled and danced by the corner of Wally's mask. The crooked line expanded into a cloud and soon red filled all of Wally's vision. He looked down, searching for the source.

Two ragged stumps swung back and forth, uselessly moving through the water. Strips of skin and meat dangled from the ruined limbs. Wally's mind struggled to fit together what he was seeing. What could have done this? Why wasn't the pain worse?

You're in shock. The voice of Wally's mother echoed inside his head. *Something bit you and you're going into shock. You need to swim. Keep swimming. You never should have gone swimming in the first place, but you must swim. I tried to tell you, Wally, but you just don't listen. You just don't –*

The words were cut short as darkness curled around Wally. His mother's voice had finally gone silent.

-11-

Lenny had to admit that the blue hole was beautiful. Things like art and nature typically did not appeal to his scientific mind. He did not like the randomness of nature or the blurred boundaries of artistic expression. No, Lenny's mind craved order and sense. But even he had to admit that Dean's Blue Hole was beautiful.

A white sand beach ringed around crystal clear water that sloped slowly towards the center where a massive circle of deep blue water shone like a sapphire. This was where his studies would begin. Dean's Blue Hole plunged over six hundred feet below sea level. Most scientists believed that the water inside the blue hole was anoxic or lacked the oxygen to support life larger than bacteria, but Lenny knew better. The same scientists, who narrowly viewed the blue holes as simple depressions in the Earth's crust, overlooked or ignored what they really were – caves and like many caves, they were connected.

The flow of seawater, warmed by its closeness to the deeper layers of the Earth, brought food, oxygen and the warmth needed to sustain life that was both ancient and new. As the people of Sunset Island had learned, the creatures living in these caves could be far larger than simple bacteria, not that many of them had survived to tell anyone about it.

Something fell from the back of one of the vans and thudded to the ground with a dull crack. Lenny groaned as he heard the interns cursing and blaming one and other.

"Just pick it up," Lenny said. "I don't care which one of you idiots dropped it, but for God's sake, just pick it up and get it down to the beach."

The other crates were already spread across the sand, open and ready to be unpacked. The soldiers patrolled the outer edges of the beach, ensuring that nosey tourists were encouraged to go for a swim somewhere else.

Cal shouted at the interns and pointed. They scuttled from one box to another, looking for whatever piece of equipment Cal demanded.

Lenny wandered past the interns and boxes to stare at the blue hole. It really was beautiful.

A series of large bubbles broke in the center of the hole. They were barely visible from the beach, but Lenny knew to watch for them. Some scientists claimed these bubbles were the result of subterranean tides. Lenny knew otherwise. Bubbles were the result of respiration, not the tides, at least not ones this big. Something was down there. Something he would have to deal with or kill before his plan could move forward.

"Cal?" Lenny asked.

"Already unpacking it," Cal waved dismissively.

A small ROV submarine sat next to him in the sand.

"And?" Lenny snapped.

"Yeah, yeah," Cal nodded.

A black nylon bag filled with what looked like tan bricks of clay, was set next to the ROV.

"Won't this collapse the tunnels if we detonate it?" Cal asked. He nudged the bomb with his toe.

"Not if it's done correctly," Lenny answered. "Not if it's done by me."

-12-

The small building, really nothing more than a shed, sat on the end of one of the docks that bordered the Clarence Town harbor. Tyde had an address from the internet, but none of the clapboard structures had numbers. Eventually, and with a great deal of groaning from Wendy, Tyde found M & J Diving Adventures. He banged his fist against the door, but no one answered. Peering through one of the dingy windows Tyde saw that the one room building was empty. Diving gear was strewn about the inside, haphazardly piled along the walls. A boat that looked like it had seen its best days in the early 1970's was moored to the end of the dock, bobbing gently in the waves that rolled in. The sun dipped into the ocean, turning the surface to stained glass.

"It's beautiful, isn't?" Tyde asked. He reached for Wendy and tried to pull her close, to wrap his arm around her, but she resisted. Tyde let his arm fall to his side.

"It looks like the last time we went for a cave dive…the last time we dove," Wendy said. Her shoulders hitched. A few tears streaked down her face, falling to the rough planks of the dock and disappearing.

Tyde took a step forward. "Wendy, I…please. It was an accident. We need to let it go."

"It's okay," Wendy wiped a hand across her face. "I'm sorry. I know. It's okay."

It was not okay, but Tyde nodded anyway. He wanted it to be okay, wanted everything to be okay, but it probably never would be. Some people might say that you could take a vacation from your problems, but Tyde knew the opposite was true – you took your problems on vacation, you took them everywhere.

"So where's this guy Miles or whatever?" Wendy asked, deciding to change the subject.

"Milo," Tyde corrected. "And I have no idea."

"You looking for Milo or Jefferson?" a voice called from one of the adjacent docks. An old man wound a thick coil of rope around his arm and tossed it into a nearby boat.

"Yeah," Tyde answered. "We were hoping to book a diving trip out to Dean's. Do you know where Milo is?"

"Probably hiding out after today," the old man said. "Got himself in trouble on a diving trip."

"What kind of trouble?" Wendy asked. She came to stand beside Tyde. Her fingers slipped between his and gently squeezed. Tyde did not know if it was love or nerves. He did not care.

"Lusca trouble," the old man said. "Worst kind of trouble there is around here, but I already said too much. He'll be back around tomorrow and you can ask him yourself. I'm not one to talk about other people's business."

"What the heck is Lusca trouble?" Tyde asked, but the old man only waved his hand dismissively and turned back to tending to his boat.

"Lusca trouble?" Wendy repeated. "Is that some kind of local slang for drugs or something like that? I don't want to go diving with a crack head. I don't think a crack head would make a very good dive leader."

Tyde snorted. "I don't think a crack head makes a very good anything, besides a crack head, I guess."

"It's not funny, Tyde," Wendy said. Her fingers slipped from his and fell to her side. Wendy turned and started walking back towards the town. "Let's just go find somewhere to eat dinner."

"Do you think we'll have time to score some Lusca?" Tyde shouted as he ran to catch up with Wendy. "Maybe just a dime?"

"Maybe just a dime," Wendy laughed. It was real laughter – the first Tyde had heard in a long time.

Tyde opened his mouth to say something, to try and keep Wendy laughing. But sometimes you just had to know to quit when you were ahead. Tyde closed his mouth and grabbed Wendy's hand. She allowed him to take it.

A dull thud turned into the fanatic slamming in Tyde's chest. He had missed this feeling. He had missed Wendy. Most of all he missed them.

-13-

Dinner was terrible, but blessedly short. Milo suffered through his mother's nagging and Stan's backhanded comments. Jefferson, busy inhaling food and enjoying a meal that did not come from a tin can, was no help. Milo nodded, grunted and chewed. This was how most meals went around his mother's table. Milo imagined Norman Rockwell painting this dinner instead of his classic Americana one and almost snorted some partially chewed rice out his nose.

"What's is so funny, Milo?" his mother asked. He could hear from her tone that a joke was not what she was after.

"Nothing," Milo said between mouthfuls of food. His mother was many things, most of them being things Milo did not like, but he had to admit that she knew her way around a kitchen.

"Nothing?" Stan repeated, his brows arched and a wicked smile creeping across his face. He was always quick to suck up to their mother by picking on Milo.

"Okay, so it wasn't nothing," Milo admitted. "I was thinking about the time in eighth grade when you had a stomach virus and Coach Wilkins made you climb the rope in gym class."

"Shut up," Stan said, dropping his fork to the table and coming to a half stand.

"Now, Milo," their mother sighed. "Don't talk about things like that at the dinner table."

"You remember that, don't you Stan?" Milo grinned. "Remember how you were sick, but couldn't pass up the opportunity to try and set the school record? As I remember it, you got about three fourths of the way up the rope, sneezed and had explosive diarrhea."

"That wasn't my fault," Stan said. He glared at his brother.

"Coach Wilkins didn't seem to think so," Milo continued. "Didn't look too happy either when it started raining chocolate pudding on the gym floor. I think you peeled the finish off the planks."

"I did not!" Stan slammed his hands down on the table, causing the plates to jump and vibrate.

"Did so," Milo laughed. "Peeled the varnish right off the wood. People started calling you Stanley Splats. You definitely set a school record that day, just not the one you had in mind."

"Boys!" their mother cut in. "That's enough. I don't know which one to be more disgusted with right now."

"Sorry," Stan said. He hung his head as if getting caught in the middle of a cookie jar robbery.

"I thought we were just sharing family stories today," Milo said, refusing to apologize. "Right, Stanley Splats?"

"You guys have sure got a lot of poop-related stories," Jefferson laughed, flecks of food spattering across the table. "That's not normal. You know that, right? A family history written with turds? Not right at all."

Stan was around the table and shoving Milo into the wall before their mother had a chance to intervene. Milo laughed. Jefferson continued eating as if this was the most normal meal he had ever eaten. Maybe it was.

The radio on Stan's shoulder crackled and a voice rattled through the small speaker.

"Stan, are you there?" the dispatcher asked.

Stan dropped Milo and picked up his radio. "I'm here. Go ahead."

"Stan, Ms. Crain called in about Wally missing," the dispatcher said.

"And?" Stan asked. "She does that at least three times a month. The kid is probably down on one of the beaches again. He'll turn up."

"That's the thing Stan," the dispatcher continued. *"He did turn up on the beach...or at least some of him did."*

"Some?" Stan asked. "What beach?"

"One of the beaches in Turtle Cove," the dispatcher answered. *"I'm sure you'll be able to tell which one."*

"Poor boy," their mother muttered as she made the sign of the cross.

"It's the Lusca," Milo added.

"Go get in my car," Stan said. "I'll drop you off at the docks."

"Okay," Jefferson said, hoping to stop what he knew was coming next.

"Screw that," Milo said. "We're coming with you."

-14-

Flying a seaplane for tourists was not where Craig Whitlock saw his life going. No one woke in the middle of the night at the age of seven and proclaimed that scrapping vomit off the floor of a yellow 1960's seaplane was the meaning of their life. No, kids dreamt of being something heroic, something meaningful or at the very least something that paid well.

Craig's life was none of these things. But he found a way to escape his vomit-encrusted existence – a way to free himself of the mundane and become something better. Granted, this path to freedom was somewhat illegal, but Craig figured it was not really all that different from his other job.

All he had to do was load a few large canvas bags onto his plane, fly them out into the middle of the ocean at night and unload them onto a waiting boat. Was it really all that different from flying tourists around on sightseeing tours? Either job really just came down to one thing – money. American money to be specific. Craig figured either way all he was doing was moving things around to get more of it.

The men told Craig not to look in the bags, but that only made him want to do it more. A quick peek inside one of the oversized green bags revealed bricks of equally green bills wrapped in plastic. A few of the other bags held white bricks, but they did not give Craig nearly the same feeling as the green ones.

He had finally made it. Sure, none of this money was his, but he always got paid as soon as he was back on the island. Craig never bothered to ask these men who they were or what they did because the truth was he did not care. Not one ounce. All he knew was that they paid well and this was his ticket to the life he deserved.

The GPS on the dashboard of the plane pinged as a dot appeared on the horizon of the screen. Craig watched the dot and tilted the controls of the plane to head towards it. He had done this a few times before and it was quickly becoming second nature.

The ping sounded again and the dot was closer – almost under him. Craig scanned the dark water below, looking for the strobe that usually marked the waiting boat. Nothing.

The metallic chime echoed again, this time the dot was directly under the plane. Maybe they had forgotten to turn the strobe on or maybe the batteries had died? Craig figured stranger things had probably happened. But if the GPS said this was where he was supposed to land, well that was where he was landing. The boat would be there. It always had before.

The plane skipped and bounced before the pontoons sunk into the water a little and pulled the plane down. Craig pulled the throttle back and turned in a tight circle.

"Where the hell is the boat?" he wondered.

A massive spotlight sat on the floor next to the driver's seat. Craig remembered buying it because the box said it had something like the power of ten million candles. It seemed like a pretty stupid way to rate a spotlight. Honestly, who used candles anymore, anyway? But stupid rating or not, Craig knew one thing – the light was freaking bright. He used to use it for night fishing, luring sea life to the surface for easy pickings, but these days he used it to find darkly colored speed boats driven by angry, stoic men with strange accents and scary guns.

Right about now, Craig was kind of missing those angry men with their guns. Had something happened? Was he being set up?

No, Craig had always done his job and done it well. They had always been happy with him. There was no way they were going to kill one of the only seaplane pilots on the island. They needed him as much as he needed their money. It was that simple.

Still, there was no boat.

Craig checked the GPS again. The dot was almost next his plane. He climbed out onto the pontoon and shone the light across the water. Nothing.

Another ping. The dot was closer now. Closer still.

The plane rocked as the water beneath it grew darker and choppy. A massive shadow glided beneath the plane and circled around the pontoons. Craig tracked it with the beam of his spotlight.

"No way," Craig said, his voice high and giddy. "No fucking way. They have a submarine? That is so cool, so so cool."

Craig bounced up and down on the plane's pontoon like a child waiting for the bathroom. He had heard stories about some of these drug runners building or buying submarines, but they were always little tub-looking things and nothing like the massive shadow that glided beneath his plane. These guys were serious. They must have picked up an old Russian sub or something like that.

The shadow turned and dipped downwards, momentarily disappearing beneath the inky surface of the ocean.

"Hey," Craig almost shouted. "Where are you going?"

As if in response, the shadow re-emerged a few hundred feet away from the plane. It was closer to the surface and heading directly towards Craig. Small waves rolled sideways as the shadow neared the surface and picked up speed. Foam sprayed and hissed.

Craig could not help but smile. This was going to be awesome.

-15-

The water within Dean's Blue Hole was amazingly clear. Bits of sea life, drifted lazily in the weak currents like motes of dust trapped in an attic. Lenny figured that image was not too far off. Things were forgotten once they were put in an attic or crawlspace and the blue hole was no different.

There may have been a time when people remembered what once dwelled in these underwater caves, but those memories had softened and become legend and lore. Lenny had no interest in bedtime stories. He knew these things were real and contrary to what he told his government handlers, these creatures were why he was here. They were the true discovery to be made.

The government hacks were interested in a series of tunnels and caves that Lenny had convinced them had some degree of military application, but the truth was that Lenny made most of it up. Sure, there were blue holes scattered across the globe, and it was true that there was evidence to support the fact that they were connected. But true military value? Lenny had no idea. Maybe they could be used for that the purpose he had made up. Maybe not. He did not care either way. By the time the military realized he was full of crap, it would not matter.

A few years ago, Lenny reached a point where he felt there was nothing new in the world of science, no secrets left to discover. His logical mind could rationalize the folly of this belief, but he could not shake the feeling. It weighed upon him, pressed down and left him mentally crippled. He thought about quitting, maybe finding something else to do with his time.

The incident on Sunset Island changed everything. There were still things left to discover, still mysteries for science to solve and dark corners to explore. Sunset Island had been nothing short of a revelation for Lenny.

But there was no way the government was going to spend taxpayer dollars for Lenny to chase aquatic boogeymen. He had to lie, had to create some angle that would get the brass to sign off on the budget.

Now, traveling deeper into the blue hole, Lenny's thoughts of the government and how pissed they were going to be drifted away. He was going to discover something amazing. He would find something akin to the magnificent creature that rose from the depths near Sunset Island.

Lenny could feel it. There was magic to be found in the blue holes. No, he corrected himself – magic did not exist. There was science to be found. And that was even better.

-16-

After close to a dozen cheap, local beers, things were beginning to feel like old times. Wendy laughed at Tyde's stupid jokes and found herself sliding her bar stool closer to her husband. It was nice to feel like things had not changed, that they were still a couple, not just two people who were stuck living together. Maybe it was all the beer, maybe not? But did it really matter? All that mattered was that Tyde and Wendy were happy.

Wendy waved to the bartender for two fresh beers.

"Someone is on a mission tonight," Tyde grinned. A beautiful haze had settled around the edges of his vision, blurring the neon signs scattered around the bar and giving Wendy a Technicolor aura. It was beautiful.

"Well, if you don't want the beer I guess I can find someone else who does," Wendy laughed. "Maybe that guy." She pointed to an old man drunkenly sleeping in one of the nearby booths. "Bet I could get into those pants." Wendy elbowed Tyde in the ribs.

"Looks like he peed those pants," Tyde said. "Good luck with that one."

Wendy erupted into laughter and found her arm wrapped around Tyde's waist. She pulled him closer. Things had been bad. Terrible, really, but this felt right. It felt good. Tyde was her husband and she was remembering why she had fallen in love with him in the first place.

"This was a good idea," Wendy whispered, her head on Tyde's shoulder.

"The beer?" Tyde asked.

"The trip, you dumb ass," Wendy laughed.

"I know," Tyde said. "I just wanted to hear you say it. I've missed you, Wendy. I've missed us."

"Me too," Wendy answered, somewhat shocked by her honesty. She did miss them.

Tyde opened his mouth to say something, but Wendy pulled him in for a kiss. There was nothing more that needed to be said. Words would ruin the special place they had rediscovered – their own personal island, afloat in a sea of beer.

"They found a foot!" someone shouted. "On the beach in Turtle Cove! A foot! And I heard something had chewed on it!"

"It had to be the Lusca!" someone else shouted from across the bar.

The happy reggae music blasting through the tinny speakers for the tourists faded away. The locals began offering different theories on what could reduce a body to just a ragged stump of a foot. The tourists, uncomfortable and eager to return to their vacations silently slipped out the door. The alcohol-induced spell inside the bar was broken with the silencing of the steel drums.

Tyde and Wendy pulled away from each other. They were thrust back into a world where horrible things could happen. A world they had tried to escape. A world that had followed them here and was all too real.

"Come on," Wendy sighed. "Let's go back to the hotel." She slid off the high stool.

"But…" Tyde began to argue, but could see that moment was gone. He dropped off his stool and followed behind Wendy.

-17-

A foot. Just a foot.

Normally a foot would be one of the lesser-noticed parts of the human body. It was just a foot. Besides fetishists, who noticed a foot?

But a foot on its own is an entirely different story. Everyone noticed that, especially when it was sitting on the beach, slightly buried in the sand with a splintered shank of bone jutting from the raw stump to glow in the moonlight.

"Oh man," Jefferson gagged, a trembling hand covering his mouth. "That's a foot. Like. A. Human. Foot."

"How observant of you," Stan said. "I'm so glad you slipped out of the back of my car to lend your uncanny detective abilities to my investigation."

Stan pushed past the other officers who were keeping the onlookers at bay. Jefferson and Milo followed close behind.

"Well, detective dick, since you're such a pro, why don't you tell me who that foot belongs to?" Jefferson said.

"It's a fucking foot you moron," Stan said, almost shouting. "What the hell do you want me to do? Interview it?"

"Or read the medical ID," Milo said pointing to the severed limb. He peered closer. The details spoke of nothing but pain and horrible death. Strips of skin hung like the rubber of a popped balloon. Raw bits of red meat were coated with sand, filling Milo's head with uncomfortable memories of his mother breading chicken in the kitchen. But Milo forced his eye to look past these horrid details and focus on the small silver chain that wrapped around the ankle of the foot and slightly buried in the sand.

"Who would wear a medical ID on their ankle?" Jefferson asked. "Aren't those supposed to be like, I don't know, visible? My grandpa rocks one of those on his wrist because of his diabetes."

"Good question," Stan said. He pulled a pen from his pants pocket and poked at the chain, gently lifting it and turning the plate to face him.

"More like easy question," Milo added.

"Really now?" Stan asked.

"Yeah, but not one I'd expect you to be able to answer, Momma's Boy," Milo said. "Dude, it's a kid. That's who would try and hide a medical ID. He or she wouldn't want people to rag on them for wearing it, but also wouldn't want to deal with their mother's nagging."

"A kid?" Jefferson asked.

"He's right," Stan said. He stood and almost put the pen back into his pocket, but stopped. He looked at the writing tool, considering whether or not to return it to his pocket. Bits of sand and gore clung to the tip. The idea of littering was evidently more unsavory. With a noticeable shudder, Stan slipped the pen back into his pocket. "It's Wally Crain."

"Or at least Wally Crain's foot," Jefferson clarified.

"Someone needs to call his mother," Stan barked at the nearby officers. "She was worried about him earlier. Get her down to the station."

The other officers hesitated, looking over their shoulders towards the road.

"We can't, sir," one of the younger officers answered.

"Why the hell not?" Stan asked.

"Because she is already here," the young officer replied.

A banshee's wail carried across the beach, mixing with the crashing waves and uncomfortable murmurs of the crowd.

"Is this just another accident, too?" Milo asked. "Still don't think it's the Lusca?"

"Milo, shut the hell up," Stan snapped.

"Why?" Milo pressed. "Because you still don't believe me?"

"No," Stan answered, watching Wally's grieving mother get closer to the ragged remains of her child. "Because I'm starting to."

-18-

"So how's this thing work?" one of the interns asked Cal. Lenny could barely stomach looking at them, let alone speaking to them. As it turned out, Cal had some uses and mildly redeeming qualities.

Lenny emerged from Dean's Blue Hole completely exhausted – the physical toll of the experimental diving equipment was a minor annoyance, but paled in comparison to the benefits.

"It's a stabilized form of liquefied oxygen," Cal answered. He shook one of the tanks Lenny had just dropped to the sand. A strange sound sloshed inside the twin air tanks. "Basically, you eat it."

"Eat it?" the intern asked. "Why the heck would you eat oxygen?"

"Dr. Borges came up the idea," Cal said. "The human body can only go so deep underwater before the pressure starts to collapse the lungs. Even if you could pull from the tank, your lungs wouldn't be able to expand enough to take the air in. And even if you could do it, the carbon dioxide would build up in your blood and eventually kill you."

"So this prevents all of that?" the intern asked as she kicked the tank. "Is it safe? I thought liquid oxygen was dangerous to organic material."

"In its normal form it's deadly, but this has been put through a few more steps to make it safe. It won't cause any harm to organic material. Basically, Doc Borges found a way to almost trick your body into thinking its water," Cal said, "and please don't kick the tank. The way that Doc Borges liquefies the oxygen makes it pretty unstable. That's why we have to transport the tanks in those giant yellow boxes."

"So highly explosive liquefied oxygen is answer to everything," the intern joked.

"It's a little more than just that," Cal grinned. "Through ingestion, the liquefied oxygen floods the bloodstream and organs, keeping them supplied with oxygen, while keeping carbon dioxide in check and balancing out the pressure. All you do is swallow it and then blow out. We've even found that trace amounts stay in your system for a few hours and allow the user to stay underwater longer than usual, even without tanks – something to do with lessening the body's demand for oxygen. It's pretty amazing."

Hearing Cal oversimplifying his work made Lenny furious, but he knew Cal was not doing it out of disrespect or ignorance. No, Cal was just trying to score a few brownie points with a young intern. This was a dance Lenny had watched more than a few times.

Lenny's head spun and his stomach roiled with acidic waves. A thick viscous stream of vomit erupted from Lenny's mouth and splashed across the sand. Small pools of icy blue liquid sparkled in the moonlight. Small tendrils of red wound through the liquid.

"Granted, there is a downside to ingesting the liquefied oxygen." Cal used his toe to push some sand over the nearest puddle of vomit.

"Are the side effects serious?" the intern asked.

"Seriously suck," Cal smirked. "But no, other than being uncomfortable, it doesn't do any real damage. The body has to readjust and the pressure change forces you to purge the liquefied oxygen." Lenny continued to vomit. "Violently," Cal added.

Lenny hacked the last of the liquid oxygen onto the sandy ground and pulled himself to his feet.

Someone was shouting back in the main part of the camp. It started as one voice that rose and fell like a pebble into a pond, each ripple growing and gathering more voices until the majority of the camp was shrieking. The four plainclothes soldiers stood by and looked on with disdain.

Lenny turned to look. Cal and the intern were already heading towards the commotion. Cal motioned for Lenny to follow. His legs were rubbery and protested, but he pushed them into action.

As Lenny stumbled into the main dining tent, all he could make out in between the shouting was the occasional use of the word 'foot.'

"What are they going on about?" Lenny demanded.

One of the soldiers leaned over. He still had a look of disgust written across his face.

"Some local came through a few minutes ago," the soldier shrugged. "Yelling some nonsense about a foot washing up on the shore of a nearby beach."

"A foot?" Lenny asked. "I'm sure worse things have shown up on these beaches."

"It was chewed on, sir," the soldier added.

"Sea life will do that," Lenny said. "A body that stays in the water for a few days will look awful. Forget about what it will look like after a week or two."

"It was from a kid," the soldier said. "He had only been missing for a few hours."

"Oh," Lenny. He felt his gut tighten and the urge to vomit nearly brought him to his knees.

"The liquid oxygen, sir?" the soldier asked.

"Yeah," Lenny lied. "That's all it is. Thank you."

-19-

Craig could barely believe that he was about to see a submarine. Sure, he had seen an old one in dry dock at some naval boat show, but this one looked huge. This was going to be awesome, something straight out of the Cold War Era.

As the shadow neared, waves rocked the seaplane. Craig stumbled and flailed his arms, trying to grab something, but finding nothing.

The water was cold and the current pulled him away from his plane, but this is not what bothered Craig. Cold clothes dried. First impressions lasted forever and he was about to make one hell of one on his new employers. Wet and stupid were surely not two traits they held in high esteem. Craig began swimming back towards his plane. Maybe he could play this off? Pretend he did it on purpose or something?

The nose of the submarine rose from the water and glistened in the glare of Craig's spotlight. A shining mass of blue molted with white rose from the water.

The fact that this was a weird shape for a submarine and an even weirder color flashed through Craig's mind before a line split the rounded shape in two, revealing a wicked nest of tangled teeth.

A thunderous *crack* echoed across the water, followed by the whine and screech of metal. The seaplane's two pontoons bobbed in the waves. A slick sheen of oil reflected the moonlight. The seaplane was gone. Craig's mind spun, fitting together pieces of information, but failing to create a picture that made sense. What could have done that? It was bigger than any whale Craig had ever seen and no whale had ever been known to eat a damn seaplane.

Craig felt the water shift and move around him. Figuring out what was going on suddenly became far less important than surviving it.

Climbing onto the nearest pontoon seemed liked a good idea. Well, not exactly a good one, but it was an idea and sure as hell a lot better of one than trying to swim for it.

The slap of waves against the hollow pontoon sounded like a dinner bell. Craig tried to fight it, but felt the warm sting of urine as it trickled down his leg.

This was not how things were supposed to work out. Not at all. Craig was supposed to get money, change his life and start living the one he had always known he deserved. Right about now he would have traded anything for a chance to return to his life of shuttling tourists around and scraping vomit off the floor of his seaplane. Even that would have been wonderful.

The shadow circled around again. With one vicious snap, the other pontoon disappeared beneath the dark water. A salty spray of foam hissed and hit Craig in the face as the pontoon was dragged down.

He screamed. He shouted for help. Help from anyone. He pleaded for a nearby boat to hear him. He begged for someone to save him from what he knew was coming. With nothing left to lose, Craig prayed. The words felt awkward and out of practice. Snot and tears streamed down his face.

"Please…" Craig cried weakly. "Please."

The water beneath the remaining pontoon shifted and dipped downward. Craig rode the pontoon into the dark absence that loomed where the seawater had once been. Rows of teeth as long as Craig's forearm rose from the turbulent water. More urine trickled down Craig's leg, but he no longer cared. He hoped that it would make him taste awful, that it would make whatever this creature was, gag.

The moon shone, glistening on the black surface of the ocean like liquid silver. Craig had once thought it was beautiful, had felt something when he looked at it. Now all he could feel was fear.

A deafening *crack* filled Craig's ears, rattling his brain and echoing through his guts.

Then there was nothing.

-20-

Fire. Yup, fire was definitely the best answer. Some days setting things on fire seemed like the best idea. Tyde was low on matches and high on self-pity.

Things had really seemed like they were turning around last night. Wendy had seemed like she was going to finally shake off the old ghosts, no ghost, that haunted her. It was only one. There was one specter ruining two lives.

After they left the bar, Tyde tried to keep the momentum moving forward, but once they got back to the hotel room, he tried to kiss Wendy and she pushed away. Whatever had started in the bar was over.

Wendy was still asleep. She had never really been much of a drinker and the number of beers she downed last night was surely going to put her through hell once she woke up. Tyde slipped out of the room to go find coffee and something for breakfast. They were supposed to have that included in their stay, but breakfast at two in the afternoon seemed like a long shot.

The lobby of the hotel was empty, except for the painfully cheery clerk behind the counter.

"Good afternoon, sir!" he waved from across the lobby. His voice echoed off of the marble floor and felt like tiny daggers plunging into Tyde's beer-soaked brain. "Or should I say good morning?" He laughed at his own joke.

"Either one," Tyde mumbled, "so long as you point me towards coffee."

"Breakfast is over by eleven," the clerk said. "Sorry, sir."

"Man," Tyde groaned, holding the side of his head. "You don't need to do all that sir crap with me. My name is Tyde, that's good enough."

"Tyde?" the clerk asked. "I like that."

"I like coffee," Tyde said.

The clerk cast a quick glance around the lobby, ensuring that no other guests were within earshot.

"Look," the clerk said, the fake cheeriness vanishing from his voice. "I have a fresh pot of coffee in the employees' lounge and the left over pastries from breakfast. Hangovers suck, brother, so come on, I'll get you set up with some caffeine and sugar." He pushed open the swinging door to allow Tyde behind the desk. A door led into the employees' lounge.

A cheap folding table surrounded by metal chairs filled the middle of the room with a tray of assorted pastries in the center. A couch that looked like it was more duct tape than couch, sat in the far corner. On top of a banged up end table sat a small TV with some local news broadcast splayed across the screen.

"Here," the clerk said and handed Tyde a Styrofoam cup of coffee. The black liquid sloshed in stark contrast against the white, synthetic material. It looked wonderful.

"Thanks...uh...um," Tyde hesitated and suddenly felt like an ugly American for not having asked the clerk his name.

"Eddie," the clerk grinned. "And don't stress it man. Most tourists don't even make eye contact when they check in."

"Is this about the foot?" Tyde asked, pointing towards the television.

"Nothing else for them to talk about," Eddie shrugged. "Sometimes people get hurt or die swimming around the wrecks and shit that's in the water. It's a shame, supposed to be a kid this time."

"So you think it was just an accident?" Tyde asked.

"What else would it be?" Eddie studied the reporter standing on a nearby beach.

"I dunno," Tyde lied. "Like maybe the Lusca or something like that?"

"The Lusca?" Eddie snorted. "Man, that's just some old wives' tale about a giant octopus."

"So you don't believe in it?" Tyde drained the coffee from his cup and went to refill his cup. He needed to remember to bring some back for Wendy.

"Believe?" Eddie asked. "I mean, I guess a giant octopus could exist somewhere, but not around here, not like the old stories say it does. It just wouldn't be able to stay hidden for that long."

"What about in Dean's Blue Hole?" Tyde pressed. "Something could hide there, right?"

"Nope," Eddie answered. "There's no oxygen in the water once you go down deep. Nothing lives down there, except for bacteria and shit like that."

"You seem to know a lot about diving," Tyde said. "We were hoping to dive at Dean's, but I guess that's not going to happen since there was an accident and people are freaked out about the Lusca."

"My brother takes me diving there sometimes," Eddie said. "He runs a dive company with his friend. Best one on the island, if you ask me."

"Think you'd be able to get him to take us?" Tyde asked. "I mean, as long as he's not worried about the Lusca or anything."

"Worried?" Eddie repeated. "Jefferson is always worried about something, but more than being neurotic, he's a business man. So long as your money is green I'm sure he'll take you diving."

"Call him, please," Tyde grinned. He could still save this day. Wendy would love diving at Dean's.

Eddie grabbed a cell phone from his pocket and dialed. He had a hushed argument and threw a few numbers back and forth. Finally, he nodded and grinned. "Jefferson says he'll be here in two hours. It's going to cost one hundred…each."

Tyde looked up from where he was busy filling a second cup of coffee and grabbing a few pastries for Wendy. "One hundred, each?"

"Sorry, man," Eddie shrugged. "Shit is kinda hairy with what's going on. I argued him down to one hundred, but I don't think he'd do it for less. I can call him back and tell him he's a greedy bastard and cancel."

"No! Don't! It's okay, I can pay it," Tyde said quickly. He stopped in the doorway. "Thanks Eddie, I think you may have just saved my marriage."

-21-

"Who was that?" Milo demanded. He could tell from the look on Jefferson's face that it involved money. His friend had always been level headed, if not a little paranoid, but when money entered the equation, he lost all common sense.

"It was my brother," Jefferson said. "Just Eddie."

"What'd he want?" Milo asked.

"What's with the twenty questions?" Jefferson asked. "Just because your brother is a cop doesn't mean that you're a detective. Chill out."

"Fine," Milo snapped. "Then answer my question and I'll chill out."

"Eddie said there's two tourists looking for a tour of the island," Jefferson lied. "I figured I'd take them around and make a few bucks since *someone* won't let us book any dives."

"No one is going in the water until we figure out what the hell is going on," Milo said. "We're not taking any more risks. It's not worth the money."

"Is that Stan talking or Milo?" Jefferson teased.

"Shut up." Milo turned back to the workbench in front of him and continued tinkering with the faulty air gauge on his air tanks. "For once, I happen to agree with Stan. I don't think anyone should be going out diving."

"Yeah, but he closed down every damn dive company on the island," Jefferson said. "Even if there is something out there, I don't see the point in shutting down every damn company."

"It's for everyone's good," Milo said. "I don't like losing money either, but if the Lusca is lurking out there, staying out of the water is the best bet."

"Staying out of the water?" Jefferson scoffed. "We live on a damn island, Milo. How the hell are we supposed to stay out of the water? It probably isn't even the Lusca."

"I guess you have a point," Milo admitted, "but there's no reason go out there looking for it. Lusca or not, there's something out there and you know it. Just because some dumbass tourists waved a few dollars at you doesn't change that. You were just as scared as I was when we were out there, so don't even try to play big man now."

"Fine," Jefferson said. "Yes, you're right. There is something out there and it does scare the shit out of me, but I'm not about to take a few tourists out there looking for it. I'm going to take the jeep and give them a tour to make a few dollars while we wait for this shit storm to blow over."

"Alright," Milo said. He was done trying to talk sense into his friend. Jefferson had made up his mind and hopefully was not stupid enough to do anything that would put people in danger. Besides, if he had the jeep and not the boat, that would limit the amount of stupidity he could unleash.

"You want to come?" Jefferson asked. "I'll split the money with you." The last thing he wanted was for Milo to accompany him, but not asking would look suspicious.

"Nah," Milo waved without looking up from his work. "I'll hang here and get this gauge fixed. Eventually, we'll be allowed to dive again and I want my gear in working order."

"Suit yourself," Jefferson said as he walked out the door and onto the dock. He peered through the dingy windows to check that Milo was still working. Content that Milo was not going to check on him, Jefferson snuck around the side of the building. A small shed with a lock jutted out from the left side. Jefferson carefully inserted the key, popped the lock and grabbed a diving rig. Eddie told him the tourists had brought their own, so this was all he was going to need.

Off the docks, Jefferson placed his air tanks into the back of the jeep. He shot a glance towards their ramshackle building. It was little more than a clapboard shack. Surely, Milo would understand the desire to make a few more dollars. Two hundred was not going to change the direction of their lives, but it would put a little more gas in the boat. And besides, what harm could come from diving at Dean's? Whatever monster or fish or whatever ate those college boys and that kid was out in the deep water. Nothing lived in blue holes. Everything would be fine.

"Nothing can survive in blue holes," Jefferson told himself.

Had he known how right he was, he never would have started the jeep.

-22-

The soldiers eyed Lenny with suspicion after he showed such a strong reaction to the report of the foot. He had been so cold, so professional, that a sudden bout of queasiness over nothing more than a foot seemed out of character and concerning.

"Just the after effects of the liquid oxygen," Lenny snapped and pushed the soldier's extended hand away.

"Of course, sir," the soldier nodded and stepped back.

The memory of the previous night's exchange played through Lenny's head. He would need to be more careful. The soldiers already suspected something was off and surely had reported in to the military brass. The last thing Lenny needed was a late night visit from a few Blackhawk helicopters. Sure, these guys were US Government and sure, the project's funding came from tax dollars, but Lenny entertained no misconceptions about who these people were.

If they began to even suspect that Lenny was going to screw them over, he would vanish in the middle of the night and that would be the end of it. The only sign left of him, his crew or his research would be footprints in the sand, quickly lost to the coming tide and soon forgotten.

But why then had the report of the child's foot washing up on shore hit me so hard? Lenny wondered. He certainly was not the emotional type and had very little interest in children. They were just unfinished adults, waiting to mature and find new and impressive heights of stupidity while further depleting the Earth of resources. Lenny's scientific mind knew that at one point he too must have been a child, but he struggled to view himself as anything other than what he was. But why then would this report have such an effect on him?

"Excitement," Lenny answered his own rhetorical question.

It had nothing to do with the loss of this child or the grief of his mother. No, people died every minute of every day. There was nothing any more impressive or important of the loss of this child.

What truly mattered, what made Lenny's head swim with excitement, was what this death proved.

There was something here. Some long forgotten creature must inhabit these waters and for whatever reason has awoken. It was somewhere nearby, just waiting for Lenny to discover it. And not only that, it had eaten human flesh. This was an apex predator, something well above humans on the food chain. Something that refused to bow to man's supposed conquering of the natural world. This was something wonderful.

"Hey Doc, you decent?" It was Cal. Lenny wanted to slap him for making such a crude joke at his expense, but there was more important work to accomplish today.

"Yes, yes. What is it, Cal?" Lenny snapped. "Have you forgotten how to tie your shoes again and require assistance? Remember what I taught you last time, the rabbit runs around the tree and down the hole. I would think even a man of your limited capacity could retain that bit of information."

"Well, you're just a fuckin' beam of sunshine this morning," Cal smirked as he slipped between the flaps of Lenny's tent and into the interior.

"I'm assuming you came here for some purpose beyond basking in the glow of my sparkling personality." Lenny made a few tight circles in the air with his hand, urging Cal to get on with the actual purpose of his visit and interruption of Lenny's private thoughts.

"A few of them soldier boys are hassling a jeep that just pulled up to the beach," Cal reported. "It doesn't look good if they're shaking down the regulars. It'll get people talking. But Lord knows those guys aren't going to listen to me. All the same, I figured you would want to know."

"Yes, thank you, Cal," Lenny rose from the chair in front of desk. "Let's go welcome our visitors."

"Welcome them?" Cal questioned. Lenny was many things, but welcoming was sure as hell not one of them. "Are you sure you're feeling alright, Doc? You were under for a long time last night and the liquid oxygen takes a toll."

"I'm fine," Lenny said as he pushed past Cal and strode towards the narrow road that edged along the beach.

One of the soldiers stood in the road with his thick arms crossed over his expansive chest. His head shook slowly from one side to the other, continually denying whatever request the man in the jeep had.

"That's enough, thank you," Lenny said and placed a hand on the soldier's shoulder.

"Sir?" the soldier asked, unsure of why Lenny was dismissing him. "We have clear protocol on outsiders."

Lenny eyed the soldier for a moment. It was the same one from the previous night's exchange.

"You are developing the seriously bothersome habit of questioning me," Lenny growled. "Something that I'm sure your superiors wouldn't find too endearing either." He eyed the mountain of a man and watched him wilt under his gaze with a deep sense of self-satisfaction.

"My apologies, sir." The soldier turned on his heel and walked back towards the camp.

"You'll have to excuse my security," Lenny smiled. "They have been a bit on edge since last night. There was that terrible story about some poor child being eaten by a creature, surely a shark, but still just awful." Lenny struggled to muster as much concern as he could.

"There's nothing like that around here, is there?" the woman in the back of the jeep asked. A man Lenny took to be her husband sat beside her.

"No, no," Lenny lied, "of course not. Nothing that size would have any business in a blue hole. There simply isn't enough oxygen or food to sustain it."

"See honey," the man added. "Jefferson was right. Everything will be just fine." The local man in the driver's seat nodded enthusiastically.

"Absolutely," Lenny nodded. "Oh my, where are my manners? I am Doctor Leonard Borges, but please call me Lenny." He wanted, no needed, these people to stay around.

"It's great to meet you, Lenny," the man smiled. "I'm Tyde, this is my wife, Wendy, and our guide, Jefferson."

"Are you sure we won't be in the way of whatever it is that you're doing here?" Wendy asked. "I mean you have security. Clearly you don't want to be bothered."

"No bother at all," Lenny said. "I'm afraid the security is simply a demand from my employers. They are quite careful with their money and want to be sure it is being invested in the right research. In all truth, they are probably here to watch me more than anyone else." Lenny let out a forced chuckle. It sounded strange and he immediately regretted it.

"What are you studying here?" Jefferson asked. "I don't remember hearing about any sort of major research going on."

"We tend not to advertise," Lenny answered. "But there's nothing dangerous or secret going on here. We're actually researching new diving equipment that allows the human body to comfortably go to depths previously unheard of."

"Really?" Tyde asked, his eyes wide and glittering with excitement.

"I'm not much for gambling," Lenny said, "but I'd bet my paycheck that you're an avid diver yourself. We can always recognize our own kind."

"That's why we're here," Wendy added. "But we don't want to get in the way."

"Please don't give it a second thought," Lenny grinned. "I'd love to introduce you to my research."

-23-

The idea of closing down tourist diving trips, even for a few days, was not well received, but once Stan dropped the plastic evidence bag containing Wally Crain's severed foot on his captain's desk, the argument was over. Stan detested having to resort to such dramatics. He had always acted from a place of reason and fact. Whatever was going on in the waters surrounding his island defied both of these things.

"Are you telling me you believe in the Lusca," the captain sneered and then added, "like your brother?"

Stan felt a surge of rage rise in his gut. Was he mad because the captain was questioning him or mocking his brother? It was true that Stan and Milo had never been close, hell they barely acknowledged that were related, but that did little to undermine the natural instinct that demanded he defend his family. Stan figured family was strange in that way. They could be terrible – you could have absolutely nothing in common with them, maybe even hate them, but still feel the need to protect your family.

Stan filed this thought in the small corner or his mind where he ignored things that did not make sense or fit into his definition of the world.

"I didn't say that I thought it was a giant mythical octopus," Stan growled. "But there obviously is something out there and it's eating people. Milo is at least right about that."

"Fine." The captain held his hands up. "Just get that thing off of my desk. Get it to the morgue."

Stan looked at the toe tag dangling from the foot's big toe. Wally's name and address were printed on the tag, not that it was really needed – all of his information was easily found on his medical ID bracelet. An entire life reduced to nothing but a foot and paper tag. All that promise and hope gone. Now all Wally's mother had left to bury was the memory of her son and his foot.

"Are you going to close down the diving operations?" Stan asked.

"Yes," the captain groaned. "I'm going to get hell from the tourism division, but get that thing off my desk and I'll do it."

Stan picked up and plastic bag and left without further discussion. He dropped the foot off in the morgue and headed for his car. Sleep seemed like a good idea.

A few hours of fitful sleep did little to help Stan feel rested or any more prepared to deal with whatever was swimming around his island. He needed to get out on the water and try to get a better understanding of whatever he was up against.

The RBDF had boats, but Stan did not savor the idea of explaining to any of the crew members that, as much as he did not want to admit it, they may be looking for the Lusca. There was only one other boat he knew was free today.

"Milo?" Stan said when his brother answered his cell phone. "Is Jefferson using the boat today?"

"Nope," Milo answered. "He's got a few tourists on a jeep tour. Why?"

"I need to borrow it." Stan paused. He did not want to admit his next thought and feared his brother's response even more. "And I need your help. I'm going looking for whatever is out there."

"You mean the Lusca?" Milo asked. "Come on, say it. Say that we're going looking for the Lusca."

"I don't know," Stan said. "I don't know what is out there. Maybe it is the Lusca, but I want to find it and I need your help. Please."

"Okay," Milo answered. He could have made his brother beg or pretended that he was not going to help, but this was Milo's island too. "Get down to the docks."

-24-

The new diving equipment was exciting and Tyde could barely hide his enthusiasm as Lenny explained how the new liquid oxygen rigs would allow people to dive to new depths. The scientists had explained all of the new technology as best he could and Tyde and Wendy nodded with interest, but only took in the thinnest of understandings. Seeing their eyes glaze over, Lenny laughed and sent them on their way. He said a few of his divers would also be in the water, but that Tyde and Wendy should pay them no mind and enjoy the amazing sights hidden within the depths of Dean's.

But all of that had little to do with Tyde's racing pulse and the pounding of his heart in his ears. New dive equipment was cool, but it paled in comparison to seeing Wendy suit up and swim towards Dean's Blue Hole.

It had been so long, too long, since Tyde and Wendy had dived together. Memories of past tragedy threatened to shake the foundation of Tyde's happiness. He pushed these thoughts down and tried to remain focused on the image of Wendy gracefully gliding through the water. Diving had brought them together and it would do it again.

Wendy turned and pointed towards the gaping maw of Dean's Blue Hole. The white sand disappeared into the craggy azure opening and the darkness it contained. Small fish darted around the edges like errant beams of rainbow. Wendy's eyes widened as she stared back at Tyde. She was excited. She was having fun. Tyde felt a few of the jagged pieces of their broken life slip back into place.

Just like a puzzle, Tyde thought as he kicked towards Wendy and Jefferson. *This is going to work. This is going to save our marriage.*

Jefferson nodded and gave a thumbs up. Tyde and Wendy returned the gesture and the three tilted themselves towards massive underwater cave that yawned beneath them.

The interior chambers of Dean's Blue Hole looked out of place on Earth. They were cold, almost devoid of life and completely alien. But they were beautiful. Wendy was beautiful. Tyde enjoyed watching her dive again more than the dive itself.

Wendy turned and snapped a quick picture of Tyde. He looked like he was enjoying himself and she suddenly found herself enjoying the dive as well. Maybe things could be fixed. Maybe the past could just be the past and cease to be a toxic cloud that hung over their marriage.

Jefferson waved and signaled for Tyde and Wendy to swim closer. He pointed to a tunnel that led out of the main chamber. Tyde glanced at Wendy. She nodded and the three swam deeper into the blue hole.

The tunnel narrowed and tooth-like formations jutted from the walls. Tyde couldn't help but envision a giant mouth and thoughts of the kid who died drifted into his head. A strange, almost transparent fish darted past Wendy. She rushed to take a picture of the creature. All other thoughts were chased from Tyde's mind.

Jefferson turned to see how the tourists were doing. As far as tourists went, they weren't too bad. A shadow drifted into the tunnel. It wasn't anything too large, no bigger than a person – probably just a shark or some other lost fish that would soon find its way back into open water. Jefferson motioned for Tyde and Wendy to follow.

Two more shadows joined the other and the three slowly drifted behind the divers.

-25-

Milo steered his boat around the edges of Long Island. It was strange to be on the water with few other boats. A couple of patrol boats passed, but once word was passed along that Stan was in the civilian craft, none bothered to stop them.

"You see anything?" Milo asked from the behind the steering wheel. Stan shook his head. After searching for most of the day, they still found nothing, especially not a giant sea monster. Stan was beginning to question if he had made a mistake. If maybe he had overreacted and gotten caught up in the hysterics of locals, locals who were probably drunk on more than folklore.

"There," Milo shouted and pointed off to the right. A large shadowy outline bobbed in the water, slightly larger than the boat, but surely not big enough to be the Lusca.

The engines idled and chugged as Milo shifted the boat into neutral and let the motion of the water carry them closer to the object.

"What is it?" Milo asked as he climbed into the bow next to his brother. He noticed that Stan's fingers delicately touched the clasp on his holster, as if debating the need for the weapon. He unclipped the snap, but left his gun in the holster. Stan was not ready to accept the existence of the Lusca, but did not seem quite ready to rule it out.

"It looks like a whale," Milo said as the bow of his boat nudged the dark mass that bobbed in front of them.

"A killer whale," Stan added. The large body of the creature gently rocked in the waves on its side. The one visible eye was gone, probably having been plucked from its orbit by some sea birds, birds that were now oddly absent. Circular red divots punctuated the sleek twenty-foot body of the whale. Each fleshy crater was roughly the size of a large grapefruit, the edges ringed with bits of stringy meat.

"What could do that?" Stan asked, pointing to the weeping wounds peppering the flank of the whale.

"I'm not sure," Milo answered honestly. "It looks like something just tore chunks right out of it, but what could do that to a killer whale?"

"Do you think maybe the whale is what got those college kids and Wally?" Stan asked, the thin hope contained within his words snapped before the words had fully formed. "Maybe it was sick and attacking people. Isn't that what they think happened with the shark that inspired Jaws?"

"Yeah," Milo agreed. "That's what happened to the shark, or at least what they think happened, but I don't see how that helps us."

"What do you mean?" Stan asked.

"Because if a sick killer whale is what ate those kids, we're in even more trouble than we thought." Milo started back towards the controls. He wanted to get the boat moving as soon as possible.

"Milo, don't start with all that Lusca crap again," Stan snapped. His logical mind wanted to answer the question of what killed those people and wanted even more to report that it was over. "It's dead. What else is there?"

"Yeah, it's dead," Milo nodded. "But whatever killed it isn't."

"Those wounds have to be from scavengers," Stan protested. "What could do that to a killer whale that size? Nothing around here could do that."

The water behind Milo's boat rippled as a sleek, serpentine tentacle broke the water and flicked the air. The molted black and red spire glistened in the sun. The tentacle's underside, coal black and covered with rings of varying sizes, flexed and pulsated, revealing a wickedly curved translucent tooth that hid within each sucker. The chug of the boat's engines hid the sound of three more tentacles slipping free of the water.

A wet *slap* left Milo's ears ringing as the boat pitched backwards. The engines coughed, sputtered and died as they were pulled beneath the frothing water.

Milo saw his brother draw his gun and watched his forearm flex as he squeezed the trigger, but the sounds of the shots never registered in Milo's mind. His ears rung and his mind scrambled to make sense of what it was seeing.

Four red blossoms bloomed on the tentacle as Stan's shots found their mark. The tentacle recoiled and curled back on itself, retreating into the turbulent waters.

"Get the engines started," Stan shouted as he sighted the other tentacles.

Milo twisted the key. Nothing. He pushed the choke and wrenched the key again. Still nothing.

"The engines are dead," Milo said, immediately regretting his word choice.

-26-

A large, semi-circular lip of rock jutted into the water above Tyde's head. Jefferson had already climbed out of the water to ensure that it was safe. His hand broke the water and motioned for Tyde and Wendy to join him. Moments later, they climbed out of the water and shed their heavy diving gear.

"This is amazing," Wendy gasped as she ran her hand over the smooth walls of the rocky alcove. The wet gray stone shone where the beam of flashlights passed over it.

"Pretty cool, right?" Jefferson nodded. "My business partner, Milo, and I found this on a dive. I figured you might like it."

"How is there air in here?" Tyde asked. "Shouldn't it be hard to breath down here?"

"Best we can figure is that there must be a connection between here and surface," Jefferson paused, "My friend, Milo, mind you he's crazy, said something about oxygen being brought in from how the water flowed through hidden caves. He thinks there's a whole system of caves connected down here. But like I said, he's kind of crazy and believes in a lot of the old folklore of this island."

"You don't?" Wendy asked. Her question was equal parts honest and sarcastic.

"Some of it, I guess," Jefferson admitted. "But not all. Come on, I want to show you where this goes." Jefferson waved towards the rear of the grotto. Tyde and Wendy followed close behind.

The small tunnel leading away from the grotto was narrow and low, but still accommodated an adult if they crouched.

"What's back here?" Tyde asked.

"Just keep up," Jefferson motioned.

Wendy reached for Tyde's hand and interlocked their fingers. He couldn't tell if it was for balance, because of fear or love or some strange mix of all three, but Tyde didn't care. He squeezed Wendy's hand and followed Jefferson.

The narrow passageway opened into darkness. Tyde swung his flashlight, illuminating a massive chamber. Jefferson stood near the middle, his own flashlight shining upwards, casting a wide yellow disk that faded into the darkness leaking from the roof of the chamber.

"Even cooler, right?" Jefferson grinned. He pointed towards a small pool that steamed in the center of the chamber. "It's a natural hot spring. I'll go back and wait near our gear. Say we'll all meet back up in no more than twenty minutes?" Jefferson arched his eyebrows and grinned. "Unless of course you think you might need more time."

"No," Tyde laughed.

"Less?" Jefferson teased. "Hey, I'm not judging. Okay, how about three minutes?"

"See you in twenty," Wendy grinned and pushed him away.

Jefferson's laughing echoed off the slick walls of the tunnel as he made his way back to the equipment.

"So now what?" Tyde asked. "Are we really going to fool around in some underground hot tub that is probably a stew of tourist skin and STD's? Who knows how many people have been in there or if Jefferson is watching?"

"Where's your sense of adventure?" Wendy smiled and pulled Tyde closer.

***

Three shadows bobbed near the edge of the rocky outcropping as Jefferson emerged from the tunnel.

Milo would be pissed when he found out that Jefferson brought tourists down here, but once he realized how this dive would attract bored tourists looking to jumpstart their libidos and more than willing to pay good money to do so, well, he would get over it. A lot of things were easier to accept when they were rolling in hundred dollar bills.

Two tanks leaned against the rock wall. One was missing.

"Where the hell did that tank get off to?" Milo asked as he investigated the two that remained. It looked like Tyde's was missing. "Probably left it close to the edge and the damn thing rolled into the water."

Jefferson pulled on his gear and walked closer to the glassy surface of the water. He would have to dive down and find Tyde's tank before they were done doing whatever they were doing in the hot spring.

Plunging into the water, Jefferson was swallowed in a roiling net of bubbles and blind. He looked down, hoping to see Tyde's air tank, but it was missing.

Something jabbed Jefferson's ribs and a hot pang of pain radiated through his chest. Turning in the direction of the attack, Jefferson found himself looking at three men in strange diving gear, gear that looked similar to what that crazy doctor had shown them back at his camp. One of the men lunged forward, thrusting a knife towards Jefferson's stomach. The second man held Tyde's air tank and the third swam towards the surface, no doubt going after the remaining tank.

A million thoughts rushed through Jefferson's head, but none so strong as the need to avoid the blade of the knife plunging towards his unprotected gut. Jefferson rolled to the side and avoided most of the attack, but the man with the knife was trained and returned with a quick sideways slash that dug into Jefferson's side.

Reaching for his ankle, Jefferson pulled his own dive knife. He had never hurt another living creature and certainly had never killed a human being, but none of that mattered. All that mattered was surviving. As the man thrust his knife a second time, Jefferson grabbed his forearm and drove his blade through the soft meat. The man screamed, his mouth filling with salt water and his respirator coming lose. Jefferson tore his blade free and wildly slashed at the man's neck and face.

The man holding Tyde's air tank dropped it and swam back towards the main chamber of Dean's Blue Hole. Jefferson waited for the other man to attack, but nothing came. His head hung forward, a wide red gash in the side of his neck weeping blood.

Jefferson's body hurt. He knew he had been cut and that it was bad, possibly fatal, but he brought Tyde and Wendy down here and wasn't about to leave them.

The third man, holding Wendy's air tank, jumped back into the water and almost landed on Jefferson. A look of surprise glowed behind the man's diving mask as Jefferson plunged the blade of his knife into his gut.

Wendy's air tank scrapped against the wet rock as Jefferson pushed it back onto the ledge and climbed out. His body screamed in protest as he pulled the third man, bleeding and near death, out of the water.

"Tyde," Jefferson said weakly. He drummed up his remaining energy and screamed the tourist's name once more before collapsing to the ground.

-27-

Smoke drifted from the swamped engines. The tentacles slipped beneath the water and had yet to reappear. Aside from their frantic breaths and light slapping of the whale carcass against the hull of the boat, the sea was silent.

"What the hell was that?" Stan asked. He scanned the water, his gun still held at ready. Milo noticed the index finger on Stan's right hand flexing and relaxing as it rested in front of the trigger.

"Do you really need to ask?" Milo responded. "That was the damn Lusca, just like I have been saying from the get go."

A loud hiss and spray of fetid salty air erupted just off the bow of the boat. The whale carcass, bloated from rot and the warm sun, split in two where a ropey tentacle wrapped around its middle. Two more tentacles sprang from the water and latched onto the bow of boat. The boat pitched forward, almost throwing Milo and Stan into the water.

"Get the engines working," Stan shouted as he began firing at the tentacles. One lashed out, knocking him to the deck of the boat. Milo rushed forward, but Stan waved him away. "I'm fine. Take care of the engines." Stan briefly thought about grabbing his cell phone or the boat's radio to call for help, but pushed the thought out his head. If he ran out of bullets before Milo got the engines working, they would be dead. There was no time to call for help.

Steadying for his next shot, Stan remained blind to the tentacle that slithered over the side of the boat behind him. Pain bloomed in his leg as if to herald the advent of a deadly Spring. Curved, razor-like teeth slide from between the countless suction cups that lined the underside of the tentacle and buried themselves in the tough muscle of Stan's leg. Before Stan had a chance to fully process the pain and what was happening, the world flipped and he found himself inverted, staring down at his brother's boat.

A muffled growl, equal parts frustration and pain, leaked from between Stan's gnashed teeth. He trained the barrel of his gun on the attacking tentacle and squeezed the trigger. *Click. Click. Click.* The sound of an empty clip. The sound of nails being driven into the lid of his coffin. *Click.*

Stan fumbled for another clip, dropping one into the water, before successfully sliding one into his gun.

Milo yanked the casings off of the dual engines on the rear of his boat. The engines were swamped, but he could fix it – all he needed was time. He only hoped that Stan could stall the Lusca long enough for him to get them working. Stan shouted something unintelligible. Milo continued to work on the engines as the boat tilted forward.

Grabbing the engines to steady himself, Milo threw a quick glance over his shoulder. His brother hung above the boat, a tentacle twisted around his ankle. Stan howled and fired rounds into the Lusca's soft flesh, but it held strong. Milo imagined the viscous barbs hiding on the underside of each tentacle tearing into his brother's leg.

"The gun. Throw me the gun," Milo shouted as he rushed forward.

"Fix. The. Damn. Engines," Stan yowled as he fumbled another clip into his weapon. Milo hesitated. "Fix the engines or the next shot will be at your head."

The tentacle holding Stan shook, whipping him violently back and forth. Milo tried not to watch, tried to focus on the engines, but the entire scene was beyond comprehension and demanded his attention. The tentacle went rigid. Stan slammed onto the deck of the boat, the severed tentacle tangled around his legs. The severed appendage writhed and pulsed, but relaxed its grip on Stan's leg. Blood streamed down his leg and soaked his sock, but Stan appeared not to notice the savage wounds dotting his flesh.

"Engines," Stan screamed.

"What cut the tentacle?" Milo asked, unable to turn his attention back to the swamped engines.

"I don't care," Stan answered. "All I care is that I'm free."

"But," Milo argued.

"But nothing," Stan snapped. "It doesn't matter what did it."

A dark shape passed under the boat, causing the craft to rise and fall with the swells of the water. Blood, black and cloudy, bloomed beneath the boat. The lower half of the dead whale broke the surface. The tail looked unscathed, but the remaining section had been chewed and shredded.

Large bubbles popped and frothed on the surface of the water. Stan trained his weapon on the bubbles waiting for the Lusca to break the surface. The bulbous head of the Lusca, larger than the boat, emerged from beneath the water. Its massive yellow eyes focused black, diamond-shaped irises on Stan and Milo. The remaining tentacles fanned out across the water. Two were missing, leaving behind ragged stumps.

The monster's eyes followed Milo's motion as he rushed back to the engines, but the yellow globes held no malice. Instead, Milo found himself feeling a strange mix of sympathy and fear for the Lusca.

Stan lowered his gun and moved to the rear of the boat. "Are the engines working yet? I don't want to wait around to see what did that to the Lusca."

"I don't think you'll have to," Milo pointed towards the mangled remains of the giant octopus.

A head that resembled the hellish marriage between a crocodile and shark rose from the water. The head alone was easily over twenty feet in length. The remainder of the monster and true scope of its size remained hidden under the waves. Two eyes shown like polished obsidian from where they sat in deep boney orbits, dotted with small outcroppings of spikes. A tangled nest of long fangs jutted from the creature's mouth as its jaws stretched and closed around the dying Lusca. The monster twisted and thrashed, not unlike an alligator's death roll, revealing a massive body shaped like an old submarine with four broad paddles and blunted tail. The bluish skin covering the creature shone and glistened as it tore into the Lusca, which weakly fought to escape before accepting its impending death and allowing itself to be pulled beneath the water.

The monster's back rose from the water like some long forgotten Atlantean nightmare before disappearing. Milo and Stan watched in stun silence as the creature's tail, stubby in comparison to its massive size, gently slipped beneath the now silent water.

"Was that a dinosaur?" Milo mumbled. It was the only logical question he could think to ask in such an illogical situation.

"Engines. Now." Were the only words Stan was prepared to offer in way of a response to his brother's question.

-28-

"What the hell happened?" Wendy gasped as she knelt to examine Jefferson's wounds. Blood pooled on the flat rocky ledge, mingling with the salty water to create a sickly, dark stew. Wendy appeared not to notice or did not care as she knelt in the mixture to help Jefferson.

Tyde surveyed the area. It was small, all angles easily visible, but he took his time to ensure he did not miss some small, but important detail. His eyes fell upon a huddled form on the edge of the stone outcropping.

A man wheezed and rolled towards Tyde and Wendy. He was bloodied and wet from the dive, but recognizable as the man who stopped Jefferson's jeep as they tried to drive to Dean's. Had this man been warning them? If that was the case, then why was he now here, slick with blood and gasping like a fish?

"Careful," Jefferson said to Wendy, his voice thin and weak. "Tell Tyde to be careful."

"Tyde," Wendy said, her voice coming out louder than she intended and echoing off the walls. "Be careful. Jefferson says to be careful."

"Got it," Tyde answered. As he crept towards the man, he noticed that his and Wendy's air tanks were missing.

"Help me," the man coughed.

Tyde kept his distance. "What are you doing down here? Where are our air tanks?"

"Just help me," the man implored. He was refusing to answer the questions. An alarm sounded within Tyde's head.

"I can't help you if I don't have my air tank," Tyde said honestly. "Without that, we're both screwed. So tell me where it went."

"It's gone," the man answered. "It sunk."

"Well then, like I said, we're both screwed," Tyde said.

"Take my tank," the man offered. "It's better than yours anyway. Just swallow instead of breathing. Just like a drink."

"Swallow?" Tyde inched forward. "Is that one of those experimental tanks that Lenny told us about?"

"Lenny?" the man laughed before falling into a fit of coughing. "You mean Doctor Borges. Yes, it's one of his tanks. He's the fucking reason we're down here."

"What are you talking about?" Tyde demanded.

Jefferson whispered the story of what transpired to Wendy as she kept pressure on his wounds and tried to slow the bleeding.

"They attacked Jefferson," Wendy shouted to her husband. "Tyde, be careful."

"Start talking," Tyde demanded. He had never been the tough guy, the one to start bar fights or intimidate others. No, Tyde was more comfortable getting by on humor and avoidance. There had only been one time he allowed his anger to get the best of him and it had almost cost him his marriage. He would not make that mistake again.

"Fine. Whatever," the man coughed. "It's not like it matters. The longer we're here, the more blood there is going to be in the water, which is exactly why Doctor Borges sent us down here. He wants to attract whatever is living down here, whatever has been eating people around the island."

"Are you fucking serious?" Tyde snapped. "You were going to use us for chum to get some shark or something to come around?"

"Shark?" the man laughed. "Kid, you have no idea what's down here, no idea what has been hiding in these caves."

"What?" Tyde asked, his nerve faltering.

The man slipped out of his diving gear and pushed it towards Tyde revealing a series of large wounds. He was never getting out of here, Tyde saw it and the man saw it in Tyde's face. "Shit, I guess it's worse than I thought. Have you ever heard of Sunset Island?"

"Yeah," Tyde said. "Some island that was destroyed by a hurricane about two years ago. And then there were all sorts of wild conspiracy theories. So what?"

"It wasn't a hurricane and some of those theories aren't conspiracies," the man continued. "The hurricane damaged a lot of the island, but whatever was in the water near Sunset Island is what killed most of those people. Something woke up near Sunset, something hungry."

"And that's here?" Tyde snapped. "That's what you came down here to feed us to?"

"No, it's probably not the same creature," the man clarified. "The government believes that that organism was destroyed by one of the Sunset locals."

"Great. That's terribly reassuring," Tyde said. "Tell me how this damn thing works so we can get out of here."

The man went over the basics. The set up was similar to what Tyde was used to, but it was still unsettling to harness the experimental equipment to his back.

"What about us?" Wendy asked. "We're still short a tank."

"Leave me," Jefferson said. "It's too late anyway."

"No," Wendy said. "I'll wear your rig and you use the buddy breather. Just hang on to me and I'll swim for both of us. Tyde will lead us back out and make sure we're safe."

"What about that asshole?" Jefferson asked, pointing to the man who had attacked him. He was angry, felt no remorse for having stabbed the man and killed the other, but the idea of leaving him here to be eaten still didn't sit right with Jefferson.

"We can leave him," Tyde said.

"Tyde?" Wendy asked. She looked shocked by her husband's callous response.

"He's dead," Tyde clarified. "Get Jefferson's air tanks on and let's go. I'm not sure what that Doctor thinks is down here, but I don't think we should wait around to find out."

Jefferson groaned as Wendy shifted the straps off his shoulders and moved the air tanks onto her back. She adjusted the set up. It was heavier than what she was used to, but it would work.

"Come on," Tyde said, helping Jefferson off the ground. Wendy passed him the secondary respirator.

The three slipped into the dark water, unsure of what waited beneath its glassy surface, but certain that they did not want to wait around long enough to find out.

-29-

The docks were empty. Milo pulled his boat up alongside the small shack that he and Jefferson called their business. The jeep was still missing, so was Jefferson. He should have been back by now.

Stan grabbed the slippery length of tentacle from where it was coiled in the bottom of the boat and leapt onto the dock. His injuries were painful, but not serious.

"We need to go to the station," Stan said as he started down the dock.

"Wait," Milo called to his brother. "Jefferson is still missing. He took two tourists out on a jeep tour this morning."

"Jeep tour?" Stan sighed.

"Shit," Milo groaned and headed for the dive locker. He slipped his key into the padlock and opened the doors. Jefferson's dive gear was missing.

"Where'd he go?" Stan demanded. "Where did he take those tourists diving?"

"I've got no idea," Milo said honestly, "but I think I know someone who might."

Stan tossed the length of coiled tentacle into the trunk of his cruiser as Milo climbed into the front seat and began dialing. Slime leaked from the revolting appendage and a rank, fishy smell began to permeate the vehicle. A creature of habit and training, Stan checked all of his mirrors before buckling his seat belt.

A small black dot crested the horizon and headed towards the island. At first Stan wrote it off as a large bird or maybe a small plane, but as the second and then third and fourth dot emerged he knew it was none of those things.

"Seat belt," Stan barked. Milo tucked his cell phone between his cheek and his shoulder as he fumbled the buckle into place.

The rotors of the helicopters frantically beat against the sky as they flew towards the island. More trailed behind, flying above a flotilla of unmarked black ships.

-30-

Eddie's cell phone rang for the sixth time. It was Milo again. Normally Eddie would have picked up after the first or second call, but his manager was watching him and had already chewed him out once this week for using his cell phone during work hours.

"Gotta drop a deuce boss man," Eddie grinned as he headed for the bathroom in the main lobby.

"I don't need details," his manager replied and went back to checking reservations on the computer located at the main desk.

"Details?" Eddie laughed. "Sure, I'll take a picture for you. Maybe we can post it to the hotel's site."

His manager mumbled something about being docked a day's pay, but Eddie paid it no mind. They were always threatening something, but never following through. Eddie was far from the perfect employee, but he was likable and that went a lot further than work ethic when your bottom line was based on making tourists smile and post good reviews online.

Once he was safely inside the bathroom, Eddie pulled his cell phone free from the front pocket of his pants. He was about to call Milo back, but a seventh call was already coming through.

"Milo? Hello?" Eddie answered his phone. "What's going on, man?"

"Where the hell have you been?" Milo snapped.

"It's nice to hear from you as well," Eddie said. "My day has been nice, thank you for asking."

"Eddie shut up and tell me where Jefferson went this morning," Milo demanded.

"Come on, Milo," Eddie stalled. "You know I can't rat out my brother."

"Tell me now or I'm sending Stan to the hotel in full uniform to ask you there," Milo said. "I'm sure that will go over well."

Eddie sighed. Milo could be as big a hard ass as his brother. "Man, look he took two tourists out on a day trip, okay?"

"Yeah, I know," Milo cut in. "He took them on a jeep tour, but they should have been back and his tanks are missing out of the dive locker."

"Jeep tour?" Eddie asked. "I don't know what he told you, but it wasn't a jeep tour. He took them diving at Dean's Blue Hole. Aren't they back yet?"

"No," Milo answered. "Get your shit together and meet us out front in ten minutes."

"Dude, I'm working a double today," Eddie protested.

"Find some way to get out of it," Milo said. "Jefferson's life might depend on it."

"Alright," Eddie said. "I'll see you in ten."

After hanging up his cell phone, Eddie strode back into the lobby, a hand gingerly clutching his gut.

"Diarrhea," Eddie announced. "I've got diarrhea, boss man. I gotta go home and deal with my explosive diarrhea."

-31-

The magic of Dean's had vanished. The rock formations and strange life forms no longer inspired wonder and awe within Tyde. Every shadow and flicker of movement spoke of unknown dangers, whispered of things that should not exist. These things were here because no man was ever supposed to be. This was a hostile alien landscape and Tyde was an intruder.

Wendy and Jefferson swam slowly behind Tyde as he led them back into the main chamber of Dean's Blue Hole. Every so often he would have to swim back and help Jefferson so Wendy could swim a little faster. Blood spiraled in dark tendrils from the wounds that crisscrossed Jefferson's body. Tyde didn't know what this monster looked like or ate, but he knew sharks could smell blood in the water and figured it wasn't too far of a leap to assume the creature could too.

Thoughts of more human attackers and inhuman monsters flooded his mind, but Tyde tried to remain focused on Wendy and his need to get her to safety. This trip, and more specifically, this dive, was supposed to save his marriage. This was supposed to reset the clock and point them towards happier days. All he had succeeded in doing thus far was almost getting them killed.

The liquid oxygen was cold. No matter how warm the water was, Tyde constantly felt the need to shiver. Maybe it was nerves and not the liquid oxygen. Either way, Tyde felt as if his bones were encrusted with ice. He imagined tiny icebergs crashing through his veins, getting smashed by the frantic *thump – thump, thump – thump* of his heart.

Sunlight trickled through the opening of Dean's, calling to Tyde, beckoning him to swim faster, but as soon as the sunlight had come into view it vanished.

A massive form glided over the mouth of Dean's, blocking both the sunlight and their escape. The shape silently hovered over the cave. It was sleek, a blunt, tapered tail and head with elongated jaws. Four broad flippers, easily as big as Tyde, gently moved the water, keeping the creature suspended over Dean's.

Wendy and Jefferson swam next to Tyde, their eyes asking why he stopped. Tyde pointed upwards and shook his head 'no.' Wendy pointed to the air gauge attached to the strap on her left shoulder. It was in the yellow range and soon would be red. Sharing the air supply with anyone, let alone someone injured and taking numerous shallow breaths, would quickly empty the tanks.

The creature turned, its shadow seemingly collapsing in on itself. Tyde worried that the liquid oxygen was playing tricks on him, perhaps causing hallucinations. The shadow, easily twenty feet or more, transitioned into black point. Tyde watched the point expand and grow, now secure in the knowledge that the combination of fear and experimental diving gear was causing him to lose his already tenuous grip with reality.

Bubbles erupted from Wendy's respirator. She pointed towards the rapidly expanding point of darkness. An errant beam of sunlight slanted through the water like a frozen bolt of lightning. The creature's snout, a molted smattering of blue and black scales, shone in the lost beam of sunlight. A crooked line of jagged white teeth jutted from tar black gums as the monster's mouth snapped around a nearby fish, leaving no trace of the animal.

The bubbles from Wendy's respirator continued their frantic ascent towards the surface, as desperate to escape as their source. As the bubbles passed the creature, Tyde watched in horror as two black eyes followed the path of the bubbles.

Before Wendy or Jefferson could protest, Tyde pushed them back into a smaller side tunnel. He didn't know what his plan was beyond keeping Wendy safe. Tyde motioned for them to swim back for the rocky ledge Jefferson had shown them. Wendy pulled on his wrist, tried to argue in the limited form available. Tyde wanted to go with them, but knew the creature would just wait them out. He needed to draw it away from Wendy. He needed to keep her safe.

Tyde leaned forward, pressing his forehead to Wendy's. He wanted to kiss her, to tell her that he loved her, but this would have to do. He turned and swam out to meet the creature.

-32-

Eddie hesitated before getting into Stan's cruiser. He leaned forward, but his feet seemed unwilling to move. Stan waved him closer.

"Let's go," Milo shouted through Stan's open window. "What's the problem?"

"It's just that, uh, well…I'm not really in the habit of getting into these types of cars willingly," Eddie answered.

Before Milo could answer, Stan hopped out of the car and twisted Eddie's right arm behind his back.

"Ouch, ouch, ouch," Eddie howled as Stan guided him towards the rear of the cruiser. Stan opened the door with his free hand and pushed Eddie into the back of the car.

"Better?" Stan asked and slammed the door.

Eddie looked around the rear of the cruiser. He adjusted himself on the plastic bench that served as the rear seat. "Yeah," he nodded. "Just like old times."

"Wonderful," Stan said as he climbed back into the driver's seat. "Now where the hell did your brother take those tourists diving?"

"Dean's," Eddie answered through the steel cage that divided the vehicle.

"Shit," Stan growled and shifted the cruiser into drive.

-33-

Lenny watched the three soldiers strap the dive rigs to their backs. He watched them silently swim out to the center of Dean's and disappear beneath its sapphire waters. The soldiers were following those tourists and their guide, though they had not been invited and would hopefully remain hidden until it became necessary to reveal themselves. Lenny knew all of these things because he had ordered them to happen. He did not relish the idea of injuring these people, most likely killing them, but he needed to bait the creature. No great scientific find had ever been made without sacrifice – that was simply the price one had to pay for knowledge.

After mapping out the most recent string of attacks, one thing became clear to Lenny – the creature never strayed far from Dean's Blue Hole. As Lenny predicted, it appeared that the animal was traveling through the system of underwater caves, emerging to hunt and feed. The scent of blood in the main chamber of the cave system would hopefully ring like an aquatic dinner bell, calling the creature back and drawing it closer to Lenny.

Prior to the arrival of the tourists, Lenny considered sending a few interns down as bait, but that would undoubtedly attract attention from their families. The tourists on the other hand? Well, they had been warned to stay out of the water by local law enforcement. Whatever tragic events transpired leading up to their disappearance would just be another accident.

Several interns were working along the beach. The water splashed and they began screaming. Cal was running towards the beach before Lenny even considered that he might need to investigate what caused the disturbance.

One of the soldiers emerged from the water. He stumbled onto the beach, fell to his knees and pitched forward into the sand. Cal and the interns hovered over the man.

"Give him room," Lenny snapped. "He is just feeling the after effects of the liquid oxygen. Get back."

The sand beneath the soldier began to darken, turning from a brilliant white to a tarry black. The interns slowly backed away. Cal knelt next to the soldier and checked his pulse.

"It's weak," Cal reported, "but he's still got a pulse." He looked to the interns. "Put pressure on the wound and get him to the medical tent."

The interns jumped to follow orders. Once they were out of earshot, Cal turned to Lenny, his eyes narrow and teeth bared. "Tell me what is going on, Doc. Tell me right now."

"A most unfortunate diving accident," Lenny waved away Cal's demand. "Nothing more."

"My ass," Cal said. "That was a knife wound. Why was he in the water? Who else was in there?"

"None of your concern." Lenny turned to walk away, but Cal gripped his shoulder and spun him around.

"Tell me you didn't send them in there after the tourists," Cal growled. "Lenny, please tell me you're not trying to bait the monster."

"How could you ask me such a thing?" Lenny asked, though his words held no injury or offense. He simply did not know how else to respond.

"Because I've worked with you long enough to know how your mind works," Cal answered.

"Then you also know how dangerous it is to ask questions of that sort." Lenny shook Cal's hand from his shoulder and walked towards the medical tent.

-34-

The creature was something out of a dinosaur-obsessed child's nightmare. It was built for one purpose – to hunt. This thing was a clear apex predator, no matter what century it found itself swimming through.

Tyde blew into his respiratory, trying to force an eruption of bubbles to capture the creature's attention. The liquid oxygen backed up, flooding the respirator and causing him to gag. A thin tendril of silvery liquid twisted away. He had forgotten that he wore the strange diving gear.

Swallow, just like drinking water and exhale through my nose. Tyde repeated this mantra in his head as he followed the direction. A stream of mercurial bubbles burst from Tyde's respirator. He swallowed again and forced another string of bubbles.

Effortlessly, the monster twisted its body and glided towards Tyde. It showed no emotion, no excitement. It was simply doing what it had been designed to do.

Sure that he had captured the monster's attention, Tyde turned and kicked for a nearby pile of rocks. A narrow path led between the cave walls and rocks. Tyde turned sideways and forced himself into the small area. His air tank scraped and clanked as it grated against the rocky walls.

Tyde watched the creature swim closer. Its broad flippers pulled its sleek body through the water, closer to Tyde. As the monster glided past the rocks, it nudged them with its massive snout. The rocks shifted and Tyde worried that they would tumble backwards and pin him against the wall.

Something beeped. It was a tinny mechanical alarm that sounded distorted and strange as it moved through the water. Tyde turned towards the sound, but could not find the source. It beeped again.

A small red light blinked on the left shoulder strap of Tyde's dive gear. There was less than ten minutes worth of oxygen left in his tanks. The alarm was going to draw the creature's attention more than bubbles and Tyde had no idea how to silence it. If he swam out from behind the rocks, he was dead.

The monster swung back towards the Tyde, this time striking the rocks with more force. The rocks shifted towards Tyde. He instinctively pushed back, but the rocks simply shifted another direction and continued moving. As the rocks pulsed upwards, Tyde's hands recoiled as if the rocks were blistering.

A long, spindly length of stone rose up from the sand. More followed as the pile of rocks lifted itself from the ground, uncurling from around itself. Two massive claws lifted out of the sand, flexing and snapping. A pair of beady black eyes protruded from the top of what Tyde had assumed to be rocks on long flexible appendages. A gigantic crab-like creature stood over Tyde.

The crab scuttled forward to meet the creature, its claws defensively outstretched and snapping. The dinosaur circled around the crab, trying to find an angle of attack.

Tyde watched in stunned amazement as the two monsters battled a few hundred feet away. The water swirled with debris stirred up by their frenzied attacks. The crab's claws snapped around one of the monster's front flippers and wrenched the creature sideways. The dinosaur did not allow the attack to go unanswered. Its powerful jaws, lined with wickedly pointed teeth, snapped around the crab's free claw. A deafening *crunch* echoed through the water and the crab's claw fell to the ground, still flexing, shell crushed.

As the crab scuttled across the floor of the cavern, Tyde's air gauge again sounded its alarm. He had less than 5 minutes of oxygen left. Tyde kicked and swam toward the narrow cave he had sent Wendy and Jefferson into, hoping that the monsters would remain locked in combat and miss his movements.

Wendy waited in the tunnel, cradling Jefferson and holding the respirator in his mouth. Tyde didn't see any bubbles from Jefferson and worried it was too late, but he knew there was no way Wendy was going to leave him.

Tyde waved for Wendy to follow him. She cautiously swam out into the main chamber of Dean's. Her attention was immediately drawn to the two monster's battling nearby. The crab had been flipped onto its back, its spindly legs uselessly clutching the water. Tyde grabbed Wendy's shoulder strap and tugged.

The mouth of Dean's felt as if it moved further away with each kick, but Tyde urged Wendy to keep swimming. Jefferson's head hung, the respirator still in place. A few bubbles trickled out, but Tyde couldn't tell if they were from respiration or not.

A sound like thunder splitting a tree shook the cavern. Tyde looked back. It was dark and hard to make out the details, but he could see two large shadowy halves that were once one large crabby whole. The other monster snapped one half from the floor of the cave, gnashing its pointed teeth and scattering fragments of the crab's shell across the sand. It plucked the second piece from the sea floor and turned towards the mouth of the cave.

Tyde's heart slammed in his chest, its hammering filling his ears. Somewhere underneath the sound a frantic alarm wailed. Tyde glanced at his shoulder. He was out of air.

-35-

Cal stood on the beach and stared out across the calm water of Dean's Blue Hole. It was beautiful, tranquil. It was the exact opposite of the feelings that swirled in him.

Working with Doctor Lenny Borges was never easy and it certainly was never really fun, but Cal had stayed for other reasons, found himself driven by the same motivations that gripped Lenny. Cal wanted to discover something new. He needed to believe that there were still mysteries to be solved in this world, that science still had a purpose. But was he willing to make the same sacrifices as Lenny? Cal hoped not, hoped that he was unable to do the mental and moral gymnastics that allowed Lenny to justify using those tourists as bait.

Bubbles popped in the middle of the cove that surrounded Dean's. Cal watched them, expecting to see another one of Lenny's soldiers emerge from the water.

A woman, her hair dark and pasted to the sides of her head, broke the surface. She lay back in the water and cradled a man. Cal recognized him as the tour guide. The second tourist had yet to break the surface. Cal hoped this would soon change. He could not reconcile Lenny's decisions and was not going to support them. He may not be able to stop Lenny or challenge him, but that did not mean he had to blindly skip along as Lenny sold bits of his humanity in the name of science.

Cal waved his arms, trying to get the woman's attention. She turned towards him, but hesitated to swim any closer. Cal held a finger to his lips and waved for her to come closer. If Lenny or the remaining soldier wandered onto the beach, these people were screwed. There was no way Lenny was going to allow this people to escape with the knowledge that he had tried to harm them.

The second tourist burst from beneath the water. It looked like he was wearing one of the experimental diving rigs.

"Swim," he coughed and belched a stream of silvery liquid.

The water beneath the three divers darkened. Cal could hear their panicked breaths as they kicked towards the shore.

"Quiet," Cal hissed and motioned with his hands. "You need to be quiet."

"Fuck quiet," the man gasped as he stood up in knee-deep water and helped the woman lift the injured man. "We don't need to be quiet, we need to get out of the water. Help us." He threw up another stream of the liquid oxygen. It hung from his chin like icicles and glistened on his chest.

Cal waded into the water to help the three divers. The man they supported looked to be unconscious and had wounds similar to those of the soldier. Cal shuddered when he thought about what must have transpired down there. His guts twisted and acid burned the back of his throat as he thought about the role he had unwittingly played in all of this.

A wave rose in the middle of the cove and surged forward. Cal had never seen anything like it. He stood in the water, frozen and pointed at the incoming wall of water.

"What? Help us," the man demanded. He turned to see the wall of water part and the scaly face of a monster emerge. "Go! Wendy, go!" He tugged and pulled on the woman's arm. She tried to rush forward, but the water pulled at her legs and she tripped. The man she carried fell motionlessly in the water.

"Grab him," she cried. "Tyde, grab him!" The man lunged, trying to grab the arms of the man who floated in the water. He managed to grip one hand.

The body of the floating man jerked back, disappearing beneath the water. The tourist tugged and pulled. Something snapped and he tumbled into the shallow water.

The tourist sat in waist-deep water. Large chunks of meat bobbed in red, foamy swells. An arm, a ragged portion of torso and a head floated nearby. A long, coil of intestine unspooled from within the ruined chest cavity and trailed behind the shredded torso calling to mind images of a hellish kite.

"Come on," the woman sobbed as she pulled the man to his feet. Both were coated with a revolting slick of gore. Strips of tattered meat clung to their exposed flesh like seaweed.

The man allowed himself to be pulled to his feet. A stream of vomit gushed from his mouth and splashed into the water. It could have been from the liquid oxygen, but just as easily could have resulted from the sickening stew that surrounded him.

Cal waded out a little further, hesitant to go too deep, but unwilling to not help. The monster circled back and snapped up the remaining bits of meat that bobbed in the water. Cal grabbed the tourists and yanked them onto the sand. They collapsed, exhausted and gasping. Sand clung to the blood and water that coated their skin.

"Get up," Cal said in a hushed tone. "You've got to move. You can't say here."

"We're out of the water," the man panted.

"But you're still not safe," Cal said. He glanced over his shoulder and saw Lenny and the remaining soldier heading towards the beach. "Get up! Get up, right now!" Cal pulled the tourists towards a nearby tangle of scraggly beach brush. It was far from the perfect hiding place, but it would have to do. Cal pushed the two tourists into the bush and held a finger to his lips. "Don't move. Stay quiet." The tourists nodded.

Cal moved across the beach, kicking sand to cover the tracks of the tourists. He moved his foot, obscuring the last set of footprints just as Lenny and the remaining soldier crested the small rise leading down to the beach.

Cal ignored the approaching men and looked towards the water. Small ripples and waves undulated across the glass surface. Dark clouds wound black tendrils through the water, slowly dispersing the life source of a man Cal had just seen consumed by his mentor's obsession.

-36-

Two unmarked black cars blocked the road leading down towards Dean's Blue Hole. Four men stood in front of the cars. They held no weapons, but oozed violence.

"Who the hell is that?" Milo asked.

"No idea," Stan answered as he slowed his car to a stop. They idled about three hundred feet away from the unknown men and black vehicles.

"Looks like US government to me," Eddie added from the back seat.

"Don't be stupid." Stan waved his hand dismissively.

"Stupid?" Eddie laughed. "You show up at my work and throw me into the back of a cop car because you want to go hunt a sea monster and I'm the stupid one? They sure look like secret government guys to me."

"He's got a point," Milo said. "Where the hell else would these guys have come from?" Two of the men started walking towards Stan's car. One touched his ear, his lips moving.

"Whoever they are, it's no good," Stan said. "They're definitely not from around here. Let's loop around to the back road." Stan looked over his shoulder as he shifted the car into reverse.

"What's the hold up?" Milo asked, not wanting to take his eyes off the men in black suits.

"That," Eddie pointed through the rear window. "Why isn't it making any noise?"

A black helicopter hovered silently above the road. A small chain gun hung from under the cockpit. Its collection of small barrels began spinning until they formed one massive, swirling black hole of impending death.

"Go," Milo shouted. "Just drive!"

A series of small clouds leapt from the hard packed dirt that comprised the road. Something pinged off the car. It could have been rocks. It most likely was bullets. Stan was not inclined to wait around to find out.

The cruiser sped backwards, shooting under the silent helicopter, which pivoted to follow the vehicle. Alarms and lights flashed inside the car's cabin. Stan ignored them and forced the engine to work harder. Black smoke billowed from under the car's hood as bullets chewed through the thin metal.

A spiraling pillar of white smoke *whooshed* past the passenger side window. Hell rose from the road behind Stan's car. A wall of fire and smoke rained dirt and rocks down.

Stan whipped the steering wheel, sending the cruiser tumbling into a drainage ditch. The vehicle listed to the passenger side, all windows smashed.

"Out," Stan barked as he pushed a shotgun towards Milo. The brothers pushed open the doors and leapt into the scrubby bushes that rose like thorny waves around them.

"A little help," Eddie cried from the rear of the car. The windows had been smashed, but a strong steel mesh still covered the windows. "Get me out. Like right now. Right now!"

Stan rushed back to pull open the rear door of his car. A second rocket raced towards the vehicle as Stan grabbed Eddie by the shirt and threw him into a nearby bush.

Milo raced to help his brother, but a thunderous *boom* and searing wave of heat threw him to the ground.

Everything blinked, dimming slowly. Then black. Then nothing.

-37-

To say that Lenny was less than pleased to see the government helicopters and boats would be an understatement. The men they contained were even less welcome, but that is what happens when you stick your hand in Uncle Sam's wallet – eventually one of those bills is going to have a few strings attached to it, and like it or not, those strings would eventually make you a puppet.

"Agent Travis Howard," the lead suit said with an extended hand. "Please call me Travis."

"Pleasure to meet you, Travis." Lenny shook the hand, not because he wanted to, but because it didn't look like the other would drop it until he did. "Now why don't you tell me what you're doing here?"

"I've been sent here to oversee your research," Travis answered. "We've been remotely monitoring your progress thus far and...have noticed some, well, I guess you'd call them setbacks."

"Setbacks?" Lenny scoffed. "Do you even know the first thing about what we are doing here? Can your little mind even begin to grasp the magnitude of what I am on the verge of here?"

Travis took a deep breath and rolled his shoulders. His fingers danced across the lump on the left side of his tailored black jacket. No doubt his gun. He maintained an easygoing effect, but something sad and dark loomed over his shoulder. Lenny thought he may have underestimated this government hack and pushed things a little too far.

"Look, Dr. Borges," Travis began.

"Lenny is fine," Lenny interrupted.

"Fine, Lenny," Travis continued. "Let's be clear about something here. We know that your theory of interconnected tunnels is a smoke screen for your actual research. With the assistance of our satellites, we also know there is a massive life form in the waters surrounding this island and that is what you are truly interested in studying."

"So what?" Lenny demanded, not intending for the words to sound as petulant as they did.

"So lucky for you, we are also interested in studying it," Travis added.

"You wouldn't even know the first thing to do with it," Lenny growled. "This isn't some creature that can be weaponized or put in a zoo. This is a miracle of nature, quite possibly a pliosaurus. Do you know what that means? Can you even begin to fathom the implications of a live Predator X specimen? You morons don't know the first thing about –"

Travis's hand closed around Lenny's neck and squeezed, cutting short both his air and words. The calm smile never faltered.

"I know more about these things than you can even begin to imagine," Travis said. He relaxed his grip. "Maybe not things like this dinosaur that you seem to have found, but make no mistake, *Lenny*, I have seen more than my share of monsters in this world and the last thing I am here to do is capture it. Are we clear?"

-38-

Something exploded. Black smoke billowed from somewhere down the thin dirt road that led to Dean's Blue Hole. Tyde remembered driving down the road with some much hope. Wendy looked excited – she looked like she used to. Tyde swore this trip would save their marriage. Now it looked like all it was going to do was end their lives.

Wendy trembled as she watched the smoke climb higher into the sky. Moments before the explosion, she saw a handful of black helicopters descend from the sky like giant wasps. Men spilled from the insides and covered the beach.

"What is going on?" she whispered to Tyde.

"I have no idea," Tyde answered honestly. "But I think if we have any chance of escaping, this is it." Tyde slipped out of the bush and reached for Wendy. She hesitated, scared to emerge from the shrub. "Baby, come on," Tyde said softly. "We can't stay here. We need to go." She took his hand.

"Don't," Wendy seethed. "Don't start with all this 'baby' shit. This was your idea – just like last time."

An invisible knife plunged into Tyde's chest. Evidently, things had not changed much, or at all. Wendy was still angry, probably even more so and she blamed him.

"Fine. Wendy," Tyde said, his words were flat and sharp. He noticed a flash of hurt go across his wife's face. Was his reaction to blame? Did she really think being angry and mean was going to make him pull closer? It had in the past. Now, Tyde simply found himself feeling empty, tapped out. "Let's go."

Ducking behind and beneath the scrubby beach plants left Tyde and Wendy's skin dotted with countless red droplets. The sharp thorns and scraggly branches pulled and dug into their exposed flesh. One time Wendy let up a sharp yelp, but stifled it with her hand. Tyde looked back. She nodded and kept moving.

A wide, shallow ditch ran along the side of the road, acting as some sort of crude drainage system. It could have been intentional or simply created by years or rain and erosion, but it was their best bet for escaping. More of the scrubby bushes had taken root in the ditch, creating a sort of spiky canopy overhead. Nearby, two men inspected the smoldering crater. A partially melted tire smoked in the middle of the road. The rest of the car lay in a heap in the ditch about fifty feet ahead.

"What do we do?" Wendy asked.

Tyde shrugged. He knew it was a poor response, barely any response at all, but he truly did not know what to do. They couldn't turn around and the road was the only path leading away from Dean's.

"Psst," a voice hissed from off to the left. "Psst. Over here. Come on. Quick."

Tyde turned to see Eddie, the man from the front desk of their hotel crouching in a nearby cluster of bushes. "Tyde, get over here." Eddie waved. Two other men were with him. Both looked pretty banged up – one worse than the other.

Grabbing Wendy's hand, Tyde crept towards Eddie and the other men. A strange sense of relief washed through him as he scrambled under the bushes and into the small natural room created in their interior.

"What are you doing here?" Tyde asked.

"We came looking for you and for my brother," Eddie replied. "Wait, where is Jefferson?"

Silent tears rolled down Wendy's cheeks, leaving jagged paths in the dirt that caked her face.

"Oh," Eddie said. "He's uh, oh man."

"Sorry, Eddie," Tyde said, not knowing what else to say.

"Was it the Lusca?" Eddie asked.

"The Lusca?" Tyde repeated. "There are things down there, but we didn't see an octopus. But that wasn't it either. Someone, one of the guys from that camp, stabbed Jefferson. He was in bad shape, but we had almost gotten him out of the water when this...this fucking monster, dinosaur, I don't know what, just snapped him up. I'm really sorry, Eddie. Man, I really am."

"The Lusca is dead," one of the other men groaned. He shifted himself up to sitting. The other man steadied him.

"Who cares about a damn octopus?" Wendy demanded. Her voice trembled as her body shook. Tyde thought about putting an arm around her, but the look on her face stopped him. "What do we do now? We can't stay in this bush for the rest of our lives."

"We're not going to," one man added. Tyde and Wendy noticed that he wore an officer's uniform.

"You're a cop?" Tyde asked. "Can't you call for help?"

"I'm Stan," he answered. "This is my brother, Milo. He was Jefferson's business partner. And no, I can't call for help because my car is trashed. Besides, I get the feeling these guys wouldn't have too much respect for the local authorities." Stan fished a cell phone from his pocket. No bars – the signal was being blocked. "We're on our own until we can get back to town."

"So what's the plan?" Eddie asked. Tears streamed down his face, but he fought to keep his composure.

"Where did Jefferson park the jeep?" Milo asked.

"A little past the main camp," Wendy answered. "Probably about two hundred yards that way." She pointed back towards the beach.

"Then that's where we're going," Milo struggled to a crouch and fished a set of keys out of his pocket. "Always had an extra set because Jefferson kept losing his." A sad smile broke across Milo's face.

"We wait until it's dark and sneak back for the jeep," Stan added. "That's the plan. Now everyone rest until then."

"Can't we just keep moving down the road?" Tyde asked.

Stan looked at Tyde like he had just suggested they try to flap their arms and fly away. "Did you miss something? They had a damn rocket launcher. They're monitoring the road. We can't just walk out of here."

"But we can drive?" Tyde snapped. "How'd that work out last time you tried?" Tyde nodded towards the twisted remains of Stan's car. "Sneaking out is our best bet."

"Fair enough," Stan said. "But waiting until dark still ups our chances."

"Agreed," Tyde nodded.

"If you two are done trying to see who can pee the furthest, I'd like to get some rest before I have to try to outrun a rocket for the second time today," Milo said and lowered himself to the sandy ground.

-39-

Cal watched the explosion blossom a few hundred feet down the dirt road. The men came back to camp, the spent tube of the rocket launcher cradled under one of their arms. They made no mention of the car they attacked moments before or the people who were most likely killed. Things had been bad with Lenny – he had definitely lost his mind and was now willing to use people as bait for the monstrous thing Cal had seen rise up from the blue hole. But these guys were worse.

These men in black suits, surely some division of the government funded through million dollar toilet seats, had just killed people for no reason beyond driving too close to camp. Cal struggled to find a rational explanation, but failed miserably and knew this was simply the government trying to clean up one mess by making another.

The one man, who had only moments before choked Lenny, stormed towards the two men returning from the dirt road. Without a word, he curled his fist and smashed the nose of the man holding the rocket launcher. The other man held his hands up, but that did little to stop the aggressor from delivering a vicious shovel punch to his gut. Both men collapsed to the ground – one spitting vomit, the other hacking blood.

"What the fuck was that?" the man who loomed over them demanded. "That was a cop car."

"Sir," the one with the broken nose coughed, "we have orders to sanitize this mess and tie up any loose ends."

"And you felt a rocket launcher was the best tool to accomplish those tasks?" The one in charge lunged forward to kick one of the men on the ground, but stopped himself and took a deep breath. "Turn in your weapons and make sure you are on the first thing smoking out of there and back to the mainland. If I see either of you in the morning, it'll be because I'm shoveling sand into your grave. Understood?"

Both men nodded and struggled to their feet.

Noticing Cal for the first time, the man in the black suit turned towards him and extended his hand. "You're the assistant. Cal, right?"

Cal nodded, unsure of what to do. For lack of a better option, he kept nodding as he shook the man's hand.

"I'm agent Travis Howard," the man said. "Come with me."

"Why?" Cal muttered. "What did I do?" Seeing the burst of violence Agent Howard has unleashed upon his own men did not inspire Cal to trust him.

"Nothing," Agent Howard answered. "It's what Doctor Borges has done that concerns me."

-40-

Night fell slowly. Tyde didn't look forward to sneaking past government nut jobs and whoever else was floating around that camp, but darkness was their best shot at getting away. He had come to Long Island to save his marriage and now just needed to focus on saving Wendy's life.

"How have things gotten so bad?" Tyde mumbled under his breath as he watched the road. Milo and the others were preparing to slip into a nearby group of bushes. Stan had agreed to lead the way back to town. It was a few miles back to town and would take hours on foot, but there was no other way.

"A dinosaur, for one," Wendy said, answering her husband's rhetorical question. "And the last few years for another. I don't know which is worse."

"I'm glad to hear that life with me ranks equal to or lower than a flesh-hungry reptilian monster," Tyde sneered. He wanted to feel angry. Wanted to be bitter and biting. All he felt was sad.

"Let's go," Wendy said, ignoring his jab. She slipped out of the bush and made her way over to Eddie and the others. Tyde followed close behind.

The path leading alongside the dirt road was little more than a shallow eroded gully, but it provided a straight shot back to the main road. Stan crouched down and led the line of hunched over people.

Lights swept back and forth across the camp. A few bounced along the road, but for whatever reason, the government suits had stopped patrolling. Stan checked over his shoulder, everyone was there. Even in the dark he could almost see the fear stretched across their faces like a death mask. He figured his wasn't much better.

Less than a day ago, Stan had reluctantly given in to his brother's crackpot theory and accepted that a giant octopus swam through the waters surrounding his home. Not only was the Lusca real and eating people, but it was only the tip of the iceberg. Moments after Stan confirmed the existence of the beast, he watched it get eaten by something far more terrifying. And to top it all off, his island had evidently been invaded by strange men in suits who found it entertaining to shoot at police cruisers with rocket launchers.

All and all it was really shaping up to be a shit week. Stan let out a dry laugh.

"What?" Milo asked.

Stan shook his head and kept moving.

Gravel crunched on the road. A car slowly rolled down the middle of the dirt road. Stan stopped. Everyone crouched down and watched the vehicle roll to a stop nearby. Two men got out.

"Out of the ditch," one man commanded. He wore a tailored black suit and had a strange pair of goggles strapped to his head. He pushed them back on his head. A gun was in his hand.

The other man wore a pair of board shorts and a tacky floral print Hawaiian shirt. He held no weapon. Nervous energy poured from him. Every glance down the road seemed to anticipate danger.

Stan motioned for the others to stay still. Something heavy dropped to the ground by Milo's feet. Stan slipped out from behind scrubby vegetation, his hands raised.

"Take it easy," Stan said. "I'm an officer of the RBDF. There's been some kind of misunderstanding. Just relax."

"Keep coming towards the car," the man with the gun said. He pointed his weapon at Stan, but there didn't appear to be any intent to use it.

"Ok, you got it," Stan walked past the nervous man and leaned against the hood of the car.

"Tell the others to come out," the suited man demanded. "Hurry up. We can't stand around here all night."

"There are no others," Stan lied.

The other man groaned and tapped the goggles on his head.

"Come out," Stan said.

Milo led the line of people out of the dusty ditch and into the road.

"Everyone get in," the suited man motioned towards the car.

"We're not all going to fit in there," Eddie protested. "That's a damn sedan, not a van."

"On a lap or in the truck," the man shrugged. "Doesn't matter to me, I'm going to be driving."

"Maybe not," Milo pulled Stan's gun his waistband and pressed it against the man's temple.

"Chill out," the nervous one said. He waved his hands, as if trying to force the tension downward. "Everyone be cool." He turned and looked at Tyde and Wendy. "Remember me? Of course you do. Come on, I helped you before. Why would I want to hurt you now? Just be cool. Everyone put their damn guns away."

"He did help us," Tyde said. "He kept us hidden from that insane scientist and one of the soldiers. Still, I don't know."

"What's your name?" he asked. "I'm Cal. I am, I mean...I guess...I was Doctor Borges' assistant. But not anymore. That is Agent Howard. He likes to be called Travis. He's here to help."

"Sure seems it," Milo said, tensing his arm and pushing the gun against Travis' head.

"Please point that weapon somewhere other than at my head," Travis said.

"Not gonna happen," Milo answered.

Travis' body moved in a blur – the black fabric of his suit melting into the sooty light of the moonless night. Milo let out a sharp yelp as the handle of Travis' gun smashed into his hand. Stan's gun fell to the ground. Travis kicked it away from Milo, but directed it to Stan's feet.

"Officer, please holster your weapon and listen to what I have to say," Travis said. He slipped his own gun into a holster hidden beneath his jacket. "But we can't talk here. Please get in the car so we can go somewhere safe."

Stan stooped to pick up his gun. Thoughts of shooting Travis bounced through his head, but he pushed them aside. If Travis meant them harm, he could have opened fire on them long before he asked them to come out of the ditch. Stan slipped his gun into his holster.

"Let's go," Stan said to the others. "But I'm not riding on anyone's lap."

-41-

Lenny sat on the beach watching the silky undulations of the ocean melt into the into the night sky. If you stared out far enough, the division between the two ceased to exist. Lenny was never one for meditation or any of that other hippie nonsense, but he did find a certain degree of peace watching the world's boundaries merge.

There had been a time when men viewed the earth and sky as separate, even believing that they were two distinct deities. Man had always struggled to force the natural world to fit his understanding. Things that weren't understood were personified and trivialized to make them less frightening. But this sort of folklore simplification never even began to peel away the layers of the mystery that cloaked the natural world. Because the truth of that matter, what Lenny now fully understood, was that there were no boundaries. The world did not include neat divisional lines separating man's understanding from those shadowy nightmares that dwelled just beyond his mental capabilities. Men were never intended to comprehend the world. Nature triumphed over science. It was that simple. Lenny understood that now.

Pushing himself up from the sand, Lenny cast one more glance across the glassy surface of Dean's. It shone like polished obsidian and somewhere beneath, a magnificent creature glided through.

A ripple and break in the water drew Lenny's attention. He hoped that he might be fortunate enough to catch a glimpse of what waited in Dean's Blue Hole. He envied the one soldier who returned. The man had been stabbed, but still had been closer to the creature than Lenny ever had. A jagged series of points rose from the water. Lenny estimated the depth to be about ten feet. The points continued to rise like small mountains erupting from the sea floor.

A curved shape rose above the gentle waves like a dark moon. Lenny stood stunned, silently hoping, though not praying, that he might see what lay hidden only a few hundred feet from where he slept. The form continued to grow and draw closer to the shore.

The first of eight jointed appendages lifted itself out of the water and dug into sand. The other legs flexed and stretched as they lifted the creature from beneath the dark water. The shell covering the monster was dotted with clumps of barnacles and tangled knots of seaweed. Whatever this thing was, Lenny could see it had waited a long time before coming on land.

A set of massive claws flexed and clacked. Two black beady eyes extended from cavernous sockets. The claws gnashed together, quite literally, snapping Lenny from the confusing swirl of thoughts bouncing around in his skull.

Lenny turned to run as three more of the monstrous crabs lifted themselves out of the water and scuttled across the sand.

Nature once again prepared to triumph over science and men.

-42-

"Park behind that building." Milo pointed from the back seat of the black sedan. Eddie shifted uncomfortably, his butt half on Milo's lap and half on Tyde's, as if he couldn't bring himself to make a choice between the two so he picked both. Cal sat squeezed against the left door. Wendy balanced on her husband's other leg, her head bent and neck craned to the side to avoid hitting the roof. Stan, the largest of the group, took the passenger seat while Travis drove. A bulky computer console filled in the middle of the bench.

Travis slowed the car and pulled it behind the building Milo pointed towards. It looked like an old warehouse, the type of place they worked on boats.

"Are we safe here?" Eddie asked. He shifted again.

"Damn your ass is boney," Milo winced. "We should have made you ride in the trunk."

"Safe?" Travis asked. "Safe is a subjective term. Safe from whatever is in the water? Sure, I guess so, but we're still a long way from safe."

"Gee, that was uplifting," Eddie said. "I was only asking if we were safe from your government friends. Like could they track your car or anything?"

"Track it?" Travis repeated. "I disabled the tracking device located in the vehicle, but that doesn't mean they can't track us with satellites. The island isn't that large, so they should be able to find the car relatively quickly. And just to clarify, those aren't my friends."

"Could have fooled us," Wendy snapped.

"I watched him kick the shit out of the two that shot at you guys," Cal added, his face squished against the window. "It didn't look very friendly."

"Could have been staged," Tyde added.

"You're right, it could have been," Travis admitted. "But why bother? What's there to gain?"

"What do you mean?" Stan asked.

"My point is," Travis turned to look at the people in the rear of this car. "That there is no reason, no benefit to me assisting you. Those people back there may work for the same government, but that doesn't mean our directive is the same. If I was in league with them, you would be dead. You have no tactical value, nothing of real substance to offer. I'm sorry but you're all nothing more than walking loose ends, so if I had the same goal as my *friends* back there, you'd all be bleeding out back in that ditch."

"Thanks?" Milo said.

"Don't mention it," Travis said. "Is there anywhere we can get inside? I'll fill you in on as much of the situation as I am currently aware."

"We've got a place on the end of the dock," Milo said. As he said the words, he realized that the pronoun 'we' no longer applied. There was no more 'we.' Jefferson was dead.

Everyone crammed inside the cramped interior of Milo's dive business. The inside of the shack was lit by the orangey glow of the sodium lamps that hung high above the docks. Milo hesitated to turn on the interior lights, but figured it probably didn't matter, flicked the switch and began passing out cans of beer from the small fridge tucked under his workbench. Everyone took one, except Travis. He set the can on the windowsill as he cast a quick glance around the docks.

"Everything alright?" Stan asked, his hand slipping over the handle of his gun.

"Yeah," Travis said, but sounded unsure. "I just have a weird feeling, like something is about to happen. I don't know. It's probably nothing."

"You think you can turn off your Spidey senses for about five minutes and tell us what the hell is going on?" Eddie said and then unleashed a foamy burp. He held his hand out to Milo, who passed him another beer.

"Yeah," Travis sighed and turned away from the window. "This started years ago –"

"Like a million," Eddie interrupted. "Uh duh. It's a dinosaur."

"Eddie, shut up," Milo said.

"Not the dinosaur," Travis said. "I meant my involvement. I'm not really sure how long the government has been involved in this kind of stuff, at least since the Roswell crash, but probably longer than that."

"Roswell? Like aliens?" Tyde asked. "Are you seriously telling us that not only does the government know about sea monsters, but aliens too? This is freaking insane. They've lied about everything. Every crackpot online was right."

"First thing I need all of you to do is accept that the majority of conspiracies that you've heard are true, or at least mostly true," Travis said. "Roswell, aliens, Sunset Island, sea monsters – all that crap is true and the government has known about it. That's where I come into this. My job is dealing with this kind of shit, cleaning it and containing it."

"So what, you're some kind of super secret sea monster hunter?" Wendy asked. "Or is the government trying to capture one and use it as a weapon?"

"No to the first one," Travis said. "The second is a little more complicated."

"Complicated?" Wendy asked.

"I don't hunt these things," Travis answered. "I contain them. There are certain factions within our government that believe these creatures have military application. People like the ones who oversee those men back at Dean's."

"Aren't you one of them?" Eddie asked and crushed another beer can.

"Like I said," Travis continued, "same government, but different goals. I'm undercover within that division."

"Our government is spying on itself?" Tyde asked.

"Does that really surprise you?" Travis laughed. "I'm here to ensure that they do not succeed in capturing whatever it is that's down there."

"Why? Because people are concerned about it being used as a weapon?" Stan asked.

"No," Travis laughed again. "The people I work for don't give a crap about the Geneva Convention or anything like that. They want to ensure that citizens remain blissfully ignorant. If people started to pull on one thread, the whole thing could unravel."

"So how did you get pulled into this shit?" Milo demanded and tossed another beer to Eddie. He was probably going to be drunk soon, if he wasn't already, but Milo figured he needed it. He had just learned that his brother was dead and that nothing in this world was what it seemed – drunk seemed like an appropriate response.

"A few years ago," Travis began, "right around the time of the Sunset Island incident, I was tasked with investigating an incident in Roswell. It was supposed to be a simple alien contact situation, but it turned into a complete cluster fuck."

"Aliens? What kind of alien cluster fuck?" Wendy asked, unsure that she actually wanted to now.

"Have you ever seen The Blob?" Travis asked. Wendy nodded. "That'll give some idea. And while we're on the subject, I'd recommend only eating free range meat or better yet, become a vegetarian."

"Look," Stan said. He pointed to a large shadow that moved awkwardly across the dock. "Milo, turn the lights out. Everyone be quiet."

Travis slipped the goggles over his eyes as soon as the lights were out. He moved beside Stan and scanned the dock.

"What do you see?" Stan asked.

"Nothing," Travis reported. "I'm not seeing any heat signatures."

"That's good, right?" Tyde asked. "That means nothing is out there, right?"

The shapes moved sideways, skittering behind a dumpster and a few parked cars. A car alarm let loose its banshee's wail as one of the forms bumped against it. The hazard lights flashed, illuminating one massive claw and spindly leg.

"No," Travis said. He clicked a button on the side of the goggles and switched them over to night vision. "It means there are four of them out there and they don't have a heat signature. Could be cold blooded."

"Cold blooded?" Eddie belched. "Like a fuckin' lizard?"

"More like a crab." Travis pulled his gun from the holster beneath his jacket.

-43-

Lenny hid underneath one of the rented vans. He pulled sand in from the sides to create a small rise on each side and provide slightly more cover.

A set of jointed legs, tipped in wicked points, scuttled past the van. Someone screamed. Maybe it was an intern. Lenny couldn't tell anymore. All of the screams had melted into one long, drawn out symphony of pain and dismemberment.

A ropey coil of intestine slapped against the side of the van and splashed to the ground. Flecks of bloody sand spattered Lenny's face. He covered his mouth to avoid screaming, but in doing so smeared the gritty mixture of blood across his lips and into his mouth. A coppery test coated his tongue. Grains of sand grated against his gums and became lodged between his teeth. Lenny's tongue involuntarily began working at the grit before a gag stopped him. He vomited into the sand and quickly covered it, trying to bury the acrid smell that curled into his nostrils.

Ragged chunks of meat slapped to the ground surrounding the van. Lenny covered his head and tried not to listen as the crab creatures battled over the remains of his research team. Horrible clicking sounds filled the air as they smashed claws and gnawed on Lenny's interns.

Gunshots sporadically cracked, but the space between the shots was growing longer. The government men were either dying off or had run. Lenny was alone.

The sounds of humanity were gone. The hum of the camp's generators droned on, joining with the horrendous clicks of the crabs' mandibles grinding flesh to create a hellish symphony. Lenny covered his ears and fought the urge to scream.

Hidden underneath the van, a cooling puddle of vomit soaking into his shirt, gritting blood coating his tongue and kinky length of intestine cooling nearby, Lenny had survived. Most likely he was the only survivor.

Lenny wondered if he had been the recipient of mercy or the one who was damned to suffer the longest. The sounds of the crabs devouring his research team would forever echo in Lenny's ears, ensuring that he would never find a night's peace.

Limbs, twisted to unnatural angles, and strips of torn flesh rained down around the van like confetti at Jeffery Dahmer's birthday. Claws cracked and pointed anthropoid limbs speared the largest of the raw, red wads of meat.

Lenny had survived, though he wasn't sure he wanted to.

-44-

Travis leapt back from the window as a claw the size of an oil drum crashed through the glass. It parted, revealing a snarled mess of spikes, and snapped shut with a deafening *crack.*

"Because a dinosaur wasn't bad enough," Eddie groaned. His words were slightly slurred, but everyone huddled inside the shack shared his sentiment.

Travis and Stan rolled across the floor, coming up on opposite sides of the claw. They both fired two quick rounds into the spiny appendage. If the bullets had any effect, the creature did not show it and continued to swipe at its intended meals.

Tyde felt something close around his ankle and an embarrassing yelp escaped his lips before he realized it was Cal's hand.

"Under here," Cal said from where he huddled beneath one of the workbenches running along the wall. Tyde pulled Wendy, Milo, and Eddie under the opposite bench. Stan and Travis continued to fire at the claw without much luck.

"We need to get out of here," Travis shouted.

As if in response or to reinforce Travis' words, a second claw exploded through the cheap wood that comprised the door. Splinters rained down throughout the small building.

The almost alien face of a monstrous crab loomed in the doorway, its black eyes protruding on flexible appendages to survey the interior of the structure. Stan lined up his shot. The crab's eye exploded, thick blue liquid gushing from the ruined globe. The monster recoiled, but flailed its set of huge claws, rattling the shack and slanting the front walls inward. The roof shook and slanted, the night sky suddenly becoming visible.

"Let's go," Milo yelled. He held open a trapdoor that had previously gone unnoticed by the others.

"In the water?" Wendy asked.

"Staying here seems like a good idea?" Milo asked.

"What about the monster?" Cal hesitated.

"What about the ones out there?" Eddie asked as he dove through the trapdoor.

Tyde grabbed Wendy's hand, interlocking their fingers and jumped into the water. They hit the water and began swimming.

The others splashed into the water beneath the dock and swam after Tyde and Wendy. A narrow strip of dock ran underneath the main pier and appeared free of monsters.

The sound of pointed, shelled legs scraped and scuttled across the wood planks overhead.

"Come on." Tyde waved to the others as he used his other hand to pull Wendy from the water. "Try to be quiet," Tyde urged the others.

Eddie, drunk, disoriented and the first one in the water, had swum in the wrong direction. He trailed behind the others. The water beneath Eddie surged and swelled. Something bumped him, throwing him from the water. A spiny claw shot from the dark water, closing around Eddie's midsection.

Travis and Stan fired into the water, but the claw closed tighter around Eddie. He screamed and flailed, beating his fists against the spiky shell that covered it. The hollow thunk of his fists echoing across the frothing water. The shell creaked as the two ragged pinchers drew together. Black tendrils of Eddie's blood twisted down the monster's arm, only to be lost in the dark water.

"They'll hear the guns," Wendy said and immediately felt guilty. Could they really watch Eddie die and do nothing? The scuttling above became frantic, almost frenzied.

Blood swelled and burst from the edges of the claw. Eddie cried out in agony as the claws two sides snapped together, closing the distance and severing Eddie in two. A second claw snapped Eddie's torso out of the air as it pin wheeled, trailing a fan of gore and flesh. The second half, spilling organs and offal, was pulled beneath the water.

Eddie was gone. The monsters were not.

-45-

The camp was silent. Even the dull hum of the generators had gone quiet, either having run out of fuel or having been destroyed by the monsters. Lenny lay under the van, anticipating a claw or pointed leg pulling him from under the vehicle. Nothing came.

Slowly, he crawled out from beneath the van. Dried vomit and sand coated his arms and chest. Lenny tried to scrape away some of the disgusting mix, but stopped after a few brushes.

Bodies, or at least had once been bodies, littered the ground throughout the camp. Mangled masses of flesh were strewn across the ground, some connected by tangled lengths of intestine. Lenny carefully stepped over what had once been a ribcage, the ribs broken and pulled back so the meaty organs inside could be harvested.

Science had revealed sights that many people would call revolting, but Lenny had come to terms with them, had found that the thrill of investigation and discovery tempered these feelings. He recalled his first dissection. It had been a pig fetus. Not too many years after that he entered medical school and dissected his first cadaver. It was strange at first, cutting into a human body, but once Lenny began to investigate the connections, the inner workings, he lost himself. The human body was an amazing machine, but organs and veins were really no more remarkable than plumbing. Yet somehow, this series of plumbing enabled life and thought. This alone had overridden any qualms Lenny felt about removing a liver.

None of those feelings or thrills came through as Lenny moved through the camp. Everywhere he looked he found death, not science. He had once seen the two as indiscernible, seeing death as the inevitable conclusion of the human condition. Now he could see his error. Death was unavoidable, that was true, but there was nothing scientific about these deaths. Lenny saw no science. Only savagery surrounded him.

A knotted coil of tacky intestine tangled itself around Lenny's ankles as he stumbled through the camp reflecting on the folly of his previous, and limited, understanding of the world. He cried out and tried to free himself of the horrid snare, but only succeeded in tangling his other ankle in the mess and tumbling to the ground.

Rolling on the ground and frantically kicking, Lenny freed himself of the meaty rope ensnaring his feet. He stood and surveyed the camp one last time. Long, sweeping marks covered the ground, evidence of the crabs' strange movements. Lenny worried that they may have returned to the water, only to rise once again when a meal appeared. But the trail of peculiar tracks leading down the dirt road told him otherwise.

The crabs left in search of food. That would inevitably bring them to the town. The people there would be unprepared, frantic. But where would they go? They were on a damn island and Lenny was stuck with them. The government agents had disappeared, having been eaten or fled. Lenny's handlers would know by now that his research had been a ruse, maybe they had known all along.

A frightening thought raced through Lenny's mind. What if his government overseers had known his true intentions all along? What if he had been deceived? Could he really have been so blind? They had known Lenny would draw the creature out of hiding, that he would drive it into a frenzy. The government missed what happened on Sunset Island, had missed the chance to study one of these creatures in action. They were not planning on making that mistake twice.

Climbing into the nearest vehicle, one of the rented vans, its white sides painted red and black with wide smears of gore and stringy bits of meat. The tires spun, struggling for traction and throwing thick clots of sand and blood. Lenny growled obscenities as he shifted the van into low gear and headed for town.

-46-

Gravity shifted, appeared to reverse as planks of wood lifted from the pier, spiraling into the velvet backdrop of the night sky or exploding in an upward rain of splinters.

Tyde ran, but could have run faster if he wasn't looking over his shoulder to watch the pier disappear behind them. Wendy was a few strides ahead. She was always a faster runner. He was always chasing her.

Stan and Milo led the group. Travis brought up the back, screaming for Tyde to run faster. He swung his arm behind and fired blindly into the planks and water.

A claw burst through the boards in front of Wendy. The dried planks snapped between the massive pinchers. Wendy stumbled, her arms paddling the air, a useless attempt to stop herself from pitching forward into the water. Wendy's eyes, filled with a strange amber glow from the sodium lamps, were wide and panicked. A second claw forced its way past the pilings and lumber, struggling to snatch Wendy from the crumbling pier.

Cal lunged forward. There was nothing to grab, expect for Wendy's hair. His fist closed around a knotted length and yanked. Wendy howled as Cal pulled her across the hole and past the claws.

"Sorry," he shrugged and helped her to her feet.

Wendy looked at her hands, peppered with jagged splinters and slick with blood. "Thank you."

"Jump," Travis shouted and fired a shot past Tyde. A small section of spiny shell broke free from the claw, but the monster showed no reaction. Tyde leapt.

Two beady black eyes, the size of grapefruits, watch Tyde's progress. Tyde, fighting his natural urge to close his eyes, looked down in time to see the second claw break through a tangled snarl of lumber.

He felt a dull pain blossom in his ribcage, had a few moments to shout stupidly before splashing into the dark water beneath the pier. Though he could see nothing and hear little more than the screams of his companions, Tyde sensed motion beneath him. Like

Eddie, he would be snatched from the water, torn in two and shredded by the tireless grinding of the crab's mouths.

The water swelled and rose, a small bluish island rising before Tyde. Two long, jointed appendages extended, holding two glassy black globes. The claws would follow soon.

Tyde kicked. He could hear everyone screaming for him to swim. He had to swim.

The claws rose from the water.

How was there only one of these monsters left? Where had the others gone? Tyde tried to silence his brain, force himself to think of nothing beyond survival, but the questions persisted. There had been at least five of these hell-spawned crustaceans, why would, all but one, suddenly lose interest such an easy meal.

Tyde's frantic kicks and panicked slapping of the water did little to move him away from the monstrous claws that flexed and snapped behind him.

Something moved behind the crab. The water shifted and pulsed. What began as a slight ripple and swell, grew into a wall of surging water. Perhaps the other crabs hadn't gone as far away as Tyde had thought.

The water fell away, a salty mist dancing lightly on night breeze. Somewhere in the distance, Tyde could hear the sound of canned Reggae music being piped through tinny speakers. Would a watered down version of a Jimmy Cliff song really be his funeral march?

As the mist cleared, Tyde could see that the wall of water had disappeared. In its place, the ungodly tangled grin of an immense crocodilian head bobbed above the rippling water. The reptile eyes Tyde with indifference, as if assessing his caloric value. Tyde treaded water, scared to move, to make himself appear more enticing or full of life. Even the crab appeared to hesitate.

A deafening crack and spray of water caused Tyde to cough and frantically wipe his eyes. The crab was gone. Two severed arms, the claws still flexing, sunk beneath the turbulent waters.

"Swim, you moron," Milo shouted from the seawall. They were safely off the ruined pier and waving for Tyde to join them.

The seawater felt thicker, almost viscous, as Tyde pulled himself through it. A lifetime passed before his hands closed around the tarred timbers that held the seawall in place.

"Climb, come on, Tyde! Climb!" Wendy motioned as Milo and Travis reached down. He would need to pull himself higher.

Tyde's body ached with exertion and horror, but he forced his hand onto the next length of lumber. Next was one foot. Then another. He was out of the water. A few more movements and he could reach Travis and Milo's outstretched hands.

Fingers brushed, but found no purchase. Tyde struggled to draw all of his remaining strength to surge forward and grab Travis or Milo. His body protested.

"Shit," Stan growled. Tyde watched him level his gun with the water and fire. He could hear the hiss of salt forth dissolving as the churning water surged forward.

What Tyde had come to think of as the dinosaur, rammed the seawall, shaking the timber and rocks, as if in mockery of man's desire to hold nature at bay. A thick length of wood broke free from above Tyde's head. He leapt sideways, but not soon enough and the heavy chunk of wood collided with his right shoulder, spinning him and pulling his hands free of the tarry surface he clung to, quite literally, for dear life.

A feeling of weightlessness overtook Tyde as he felt the world drop out from under him. He was going to fall, was going to land in the water below and was going to be eaten by a creature that should have never shared the same timeline as mankind.

Tyde slammed into the side of the seawall, memories of a failed attempt at rock climbing ricocheting through his head. Milo's hand closed around his forearm and pulled upwards. Travis reached out to assist. Tyde had always loved the water, but had never been happier to be on dry land. Wendy wrapped her arms around his neck and squeezed.

"No time for that," Milo said. He looked towards the water as the monster prepared to ram the seawall again. "We should get moving."

"It can't do anything to us here," Stan said. "Give them a second."

A shudder passed through the ground as the monster rammed the seawall.

"Just because you're my brother doesn't mean that it's your genetic obligation to argue with everything I say," Milo snapped. He was half joking, relieved to have found a moment to do so.

The asphalt rippled, buckling upwards before sliding towards the ocean. Stan stumbled and struggled to regain his balance. Milo lunged forward, but it was too late.

The asphalt moved like a conveyor belt, sliding his brother further away and closer to danger. The seawall buckled and collapsed into the water. Stan let out a cry as he tumbled off the collapsing bulwark of the seawall and into water.

Milo raced forward, but Travis yanked him back.

"It's collapsing," Travis cried. "We need to go."

"My brother," Milo shouted and broke free from Travis. "He could still be okay."

Milo edged closer to the valley that had opened in the seawall. The water below was a churning mess of stone, dirt and timber.

"Stan!" Milo inched closer, more asphalt and earth breaking free with each ounce of body weight he placed upon it. "Stan!"

A series of bubbles, large and erratic, percolated the surface.

"He's down there," Milo yelled. "We need to help Stan. He's down there."

The bubbles increased in their ferocity. One bubble, larger than the other, broke the surface and slowly bled across the surface of the water. The brownish white foam of the sea became pink and then red.

The bubbles stopped.

Charles Whitley never understood Reggae music. What was the appeal of metal drums and songs about jamming things or buffalos? Now something with a slide guitar and a refrain about a pick-up truck or a woman with a cheating heart, that Charles could understand. Unfortunately, his wife Cindy was a different story.

Cindy was college educated and from the Northeast. One of those kids who got to college and realized how 'oppressed' they had been by their parents' wealth and good life choices – exactly the type of kid who started listening to Reggae music right after her first joint.

Charles had nothing against the music itself; he just didn't understand how it was the soundtrack of his wife's life. But then again, there were many things about Cindy that he didn't understand. Charles would never be able to figure out why Cindy refused to allow her parents to pay for their wedding or more importantly, why she chose to marry him in the first place. Granted, Charles figured there were worse husbands than himself, but much like the Reggae music Cindy loved, he just couldn't figure out how he fit into the narrative of her life. Somehow her love of both things had landed them in the Bahamas for their honeymoon.

"Come on," Cindy said, her words slightly slurred, "have another Corona."

"A Corona?" Charles laughed. "Aren't those Mexican?"

"Mexican?" Cindy laughed. "They're a vacation in a bottle. Now drink." She thrust the beer towards her husband.

Charles shrugged and took a long draw from the bottle.

A department store rendition of a Reggae song droned on in the background.

"Dance with me, Charlie," Cindy grinned. She was the only one who called him that, or at least the only one he allowed to.

"Not to that," Charles said, motioning towards the jukebox with his beer.

"Then put on something that speaks to your hillbilly blood so I can enjoy my husband." Cindy planted a sloppy, beer-tinged kiss on Charles' lips. He grinned all the way over to the jukebox.

Most of the songs and artists were foreign to Charles, but he eventually found a Brad Paisley song buried towards the back. It was an older one, definitely not one of his best songs, but it was good enough for Charles. A few heads turned as Charles played a country song in an island bar, but most people shrugged, a few smiled and most didn't care. Music was music after all.

"Is that better?" Cindy smiled as she fell into her husband's arms. Charles nodded and spun his wife onto the dance floor. Most of the tourists had evacuated the dance floor when the Reggae stopped, but Charles wouldn't have wanted it any other way. This was their moment. This was about them.

Cindy laughed and tucked her head into the crook of Charles' neck. He could feel the warm tickle of her breath as she whispered proclamations of her love for him.

"Dip me," Cindy said and pitched backwards. Charles, unprepared, almost dropped his wife and stumbled to remain standing. The two dancers stumbled towards the wall, a fit of laughter overtaking them.

"I love you, baby," Charles grinned and had never meant it more.

"Say it again," Cindy implored, as she pulled closer to Charles.

A flash of stilted movement outside of the bar caught Charles' attention.

"Say it again," Cindy laughed. "Charles? What's wrong?" The mirth of her words now replaced with concern.

"Did you see that?" Charles asked.

"See what?" Cindy turned towards the window.

A gnarled claw crashed through the nearby window, ripping it from its frame and splintering the wall.

Charles leapt back, pulling Cindy into the safety of his arms. Her grip around his neck loosened and went slack. Over his wife's shoulder, Charles watched the claw pull Cindy's lower half through the ruined window. Warmth coated his bare legs and wept onto his sandaled feet.

"Say it again," Cindy said. Her words were thin and breathy. "Please, Charlie."

"I love you, baby," Charles choked. Something hot and knotted slide down his leg like a fiery serpent before slapping to the dance floor.

The claw returned, joined this time by spindly legs, and ripped a larger hole in the wall of the bar. The monster forced its way further inside.

"I love you, baby," Charles whispered over the screams that filled the bar. "I love you, baby. I'll be with you soon."

-48-

Things scuttled from the shadowy spaces between buildings. Things that should never have existed. These creatures clearly clung to some prehistoric branch of the crustacean family tree – a branch should have stopped producing fruit eons ago.

Lenny marveled at the speed of the creatures. Crustaceans never held much allure for him, but he could not help but be entranced by the ones before him. Slowing the van to a stop, Lenny watched one of the monsters crash through the side of a building, possibly a bar, and pull something out. It looked like legs.

There was nothing Lenny could do to help those people. There probably was very little Lenny could do to help himself. Maybe he should have stayed at the camp? What had drawn him towards town? Why would he follow these nightmares?

But that was exactly the point – to follow, to observe. Lenny's scientific mind remained intact and demanded answers. He wanted, no needed answers. It was a physical drive, probably what addicts felt. This could not be ignored.

A light tap on the driver's side window shook Lenny from the inner sanctum of his deep thoughts. Images of a hellish claw shattering the glass and removing his head raced through Lenny's mind. He turned towards the glass. There was no crab. No claw.

The barrel of a gun pointed towards Lenny through the glass. It was Agent Travis Howard. Lenny figured he would have fled or died with the rest of the government hacks. Perhaps he underestimated him? Or was it an overestimation? A ragged group of slightly familiar people huddled behind Agent Howard.

"Can I help you Agent Howard?" Lenny asked. "Or is it Travis?"

"Open the van," Travis said. "Now." He kept his voice low not wanting to attract the attention of the spiny monsters that scuttled through the town, rendering flesh from bone and limb from body.

"I'd rather not," Lenny said.

"I'd rather shoot you, dump your body and drive myself," Travis shrugged. "Your choice."

"As you wish," Lenny said and clicked the button to unlock the doors. The group of people scurried towards the van. Cal was with them.

"Well hello there, Cal," Lenny nodded. "I guess I'm glad to see you alive."

"Doc," Cal nodded. His fist shot forward, colliding with side of Lenny's head and propelling it into the steering wheel. The horn blared.

Everyone within the van watched as one crab, then another and another turned towards the vehicle. Their inky eyes shone under the dull streetlights. They betrayed no emotion, no purpose beyond finding their next meal.

"A simple 'hello' would have sufficed," Lenny said, rubbing the side of his head.

"Drive," Travis snapped from the passenger seat, his gun still trained on Lenny.

"Where?" Lenny groaned.

The first of the monsters was no more than twenty feet away, its spidery legs quickly closing the distance.

"Anywhere," Travis said. "Just drive."

Metal screeched in protest as a claw closed around the bumper of the van and squeezed. Travis pressed the button to lower the passenger side window and began firing at the creature. A black globe popped, oozing a thick blue liquid down the quivering stem that once held the eye in place. The crab recoiled, tearing the bumper free and casting it to the other side of the street.

"First reasonable thing I've heard all night," Lenny said and shifted the van into reverse.

-49-

The asphalt was left pocked and chipped from the tireless scuttle of the crabs. Faces, slick with sweat and fear, peered out from behind darkened windows, hoping to find the streets silent. Claws, oversized and jagged, shattered glass, severing flesh and bone alike.

A body hung from the window of a sightseeing business. It was limp and bent at the waist. A crab tugged, its claw closed around the neck, until the head came loose, spinal cord dangling from where it had been pulled from its fleshy refuge. Blood spilled from the ragged stump of a neck and crept across the sidewalk.

The crab shredded meat and tossed away bone. A pile had slowly grown next to the creature as it continued to feast. There was almost a perverse irony in the image, though none were present to observe.

Not far from where the crabs gorged themselves, a creature glided silently through the water. Unlike the crabs, it knew when to stop eating, when to leave one hunting ground before it drew too much attention.

Turning from the ruined seawall, the creature swam silently towards the open water. There would be time to hunt again. Time to consume. But something deep within the reptilian brain of the monster urged it to swim, to leave. It wasn't fear that drove the creature. It was a primal sense of survival.

The crabs continued to eat, searching through the clapboard buildings that lined the street. Bright, cheery colors, all with names that sounded like drinks or ice cream flavors, covered the walls of the buildings. Dark smears had been splashed across them like an obscene form of graffiti.

Screams had filled the air, echoing sharp and wet before going silent. Now there were none. No lungs retained the air needed to force a thick gurgle as pinchers drew together around a neck.

The gnashing of the crabs' mandibles and claws filled the silence, a hellish backing track for the canned Reggae that still droned from some forgotten speaker.

-50-

"Care to tell me where we are going?" Lenny asked. He had driven the van out of town and now idled on the shoulder of a dirt road.

Travis raised his gun, as if considering whether or not to shoot Lenny. Milo's hand pushed the barrel of the gun.

"Go to the police station," Milo said. Pain cracked his words, made them jagged and cutting. He was going to stick with Stan's plan, even if Stan was gone.

"Back in town?" Lenny asked. "Doesn't that somewhat defeat the purpose of driving away from the creatures that are presently eating people?"

Tyde, Wendy and Cal shared a look.

"I hate to say that I agree with Doc Borges," Cal said, "but I'm not sure that's the best idea…no offense, Milo."

"I'm open to other ideas," Milo replied. "Anyone else know where we can get weapons and keys to a boat fast enough to outrun that thing in the water?"

"He's right," Tyde added.

"Right about the weapons," Lenny said. "But I'm not so sure about the boat idea. That creature, that beautiful creature, is an apex predator. It is designed with one purpose, to hunt. I don't think there is a boat in the RBDF fleet that is safe enough to attempt an escape."

"We should stay out of the water," Wendy said. She shot a quick glance at Tyde. He couldn't tell if it was accusatory or cautionary.

"No, quite the opposite," Lenny said. "We need to go in the water if we have any chance of escaping."

"Are you insane as well as an asshole?" Travis punctuated his question with a thrust of his handgun.

"Perhaps," Lenny shrugged, showing no offense from the Agent's question. "But my point is, that any craft that is possibly fast enough will be too small and any one that is large enough will be too slow. The creature will catch us either way."

"So what are you saying?" Tyde demanded. "That we swim?"

"At first," Lenny answered. "We'll have to trap or at least slow the creature down so we can escape."

"How exactly do you propose we do that?" Travis asked.

"We'll need to split up," Lenny said. "Some of us go to the police station to get weapons and keys for a boat. The rest of us will need to return to Dean's and attempt to trap the monster." Lenny did not like using the word 'monster' to describe the magnificent creature that swam through the waters surrounding Long Island, but he needed to get the peons to go along with his plan.

"You want us to go diving?" Wendy scoffed. "In Dean's, with the monster and the giant crabs?"

"Well, I do believe that the crabs are somewhat preoccupied right now," Lenny chuckled. His humor sent acidic knots roiling through the guts of the occupants inside the van.

"Who goes?" Travis asked.

"I'll do the dive," Milo offered.

"No," Travis answered. "You're the only one with any knowledge of the police station. You know where they keep the keys and weapons."

"I'll do it," Tyde offered. "I don't know how to shoot a gun, so I'm no help at the police station."

"Tyde?" Wendy asked.

"It's okay," he added and squeezed her hand.

"Then I'm going too," Wendy said.

"No." Tyde was firm in his resolve, even though he knew his wife had already made up her mind.

"I guess that settles it," Lenny said. "I'll go with our tourist friends. Cal, you should accompany Travis and our deadlocked friend to the police station. Perhaps you can make yourself useful by carrying something."

"Hey, Doc?" Cal asked. "Remember how you used to make me pack your things when we'd leave a research site?"

"And?" Lenny asked. "Is this really the time to discuss the banal nature of being an assistant because genetics rendered you incapable of becoming a lead researcher?"

"Nope," Cal grinned. "But in case something happens to me and I don't come back, I wanted to be sure to tell you that every time I packed your toothbrush, I would dip it in the toilet. That's all."

"Classy until the end," Lenny said.

"Enough. Let's go," Travis said. "Drop us off at the police station and then haul ass back to Dean's."

-51-

Milo stopped just inside of the double glass doors that fronted the RBDF station. He had been through those doors more times than he could remember, sometimes in handcuffs, but it had never struck him as hard as it currently did. He never realized that all of the other times he had expected, no counted on, one thing – Stan. His brother. Who was now gone. Eaten by that fucking monster.

The station was empty. The neon lights were still on, though a few blinked as if they too were considering abandoning their post. The lights went out. Darkness spilled through the station.

"Sorry," Travis said, seeing the surprise on Milo and Cal's faces. "Thought it might not be a good idea to leave the lights on. It might attract the crabs."

"Right," Milo nodded. "Good thinking."

Cal shuffled towards the back of the station. A row of cells lined the far wall.

"They're all empty," Cal reported.

"I'm sure one the officers figured out what was going on that they let people go," Travis said.

"They're empty most of the time anyway," Milo clarified. "Most of the time it's just a couple of drunks or a tourist that got in a fist fight. Not much happens around here…or at least it didn't used to." Milo walked over towards the captain's office. He tried the doorknob. It was locked.

"Here, let me try," Travis said. He pulled a knife from his pocket and flicked the blade open. Kneeling down, Travis wedged the blade between the door and the jamb.

A gunshot cracked. The frosted glass of the door webbed and shattered above Travis' head. A second shot tore a chunk of wood out of the door.

"Stop shooting," Milo called.

"Go away," a voice called.

"We're just here for the keys," Milo said. "We're not going to hurt you."

Travis had his gun out and motioned towards the door.

"Not going to happen," the voice answered. "No one is coming in and I'm not coming out. Go away."

"Just open the door," Milo began.

Travis crouched and angled his gun towards the cracked glass. He fired two quick shots into the office before throwing his shoulder against the door.

The wood splintered and tore away from the jamb.

"On the floor," Travis shouted as came out of a roll to a kneeling position.

Someone moved behind the desk.

"Push your gun out," Travis commanded.

"I'm an officer," the voice said. "I'm not giving up my weapon."

"Well, I'm a government agent." Travis said. "So how about we stop shooting at each other? Stand up slowly and keep your arms raised. Officer or not, you do anything squirrelly and I'll drop you."

"Okay, okay," the voice said. Someone slowly climbed out from behind the desk.

"Captain?" Milo asked, peering around the ruined door. "Why the hell were you shooting at us?"

"Milo?" the captain asked. "Where's Stan?"

"Gone," Milo said. His eyes drifted towards the floor.

"Like everyone else," the captain said. "The other officers were helping get people to safety, but those things climbed out of the water and…and…well, no one is left. Just me." The captain paused. "I ran. I'm not proud of that, but screw it. Why should I lie now? I was scared."

"I'm sure everyone was," Cal added, not intending to rub salt in the captain's wounds. "Sorry."

"Here, Milo." The captain tossed a ring of keys across the room. "The large brass one opens the weapons locker. You'll find keys for the vehicles on the pegboard outside the locker. Take whatever you want."

"Aren't you coming with us?" Cal asked when he saw the captain was still behind the desk.

"I'm not going back out there," the captain said. "Not after what I saw. I can't. I know you probably think I'm a coward. I guess that I am, but I'm not going out there again."

"It doesn't matter what we think," Milo said. "Stop being stupid and let's go."

"No," the captain said firmly.

"He's made up his mind," Travis said. There were times when you could negotiate, try to save people from themselves. This was no one of them.

Travis led the other two out of the captain's office.

"Hey, Milo," the captain called. "Your brother, he was a good officer – a great one. He tried to warn me. I'm sorry I didn't listen. Maybe he'd still be here if I had."

"It's not your fault," Milo said. "But thanks for saying the other stuff. Be safe, okay?"

"You too," the captain said.

-52-

Tyde tried to ignore the clotted, cold lumps scattered across the camp. These mangled things had once been living, breathing humans. Probably just some interns looking to pad their resumes and score a few bonus credits by working for Lenny over the summer.

Meat. Now that's all they were. There was nothing human about the mangled piles of stringy flesh and bone. Expect there was.

A finger pointed from the end of a ragged length of sand-coated meat. To where, Tyde could only guess. Certainly not to safety. More likely the finger pointed towards Tyde and Lenny. Pointed towards people that shouldn't have been alive. Pointed towards people who were guilty.

"This is too much," Wendy gagged as she made her way towards the beach. She had an experimental diving rig slung over her shoulder. "I can't believe we're doing this again…you said this was over, Tyde. You promised me."

"I know," Tyde protested. His words were weak and fell apart the minute they passed his lips. He watched Wendy walk further away, unsure of how to make her stop. "This was supposed to save our marriage," Tyde muttered.

"Save it?" Lenny snorted. "Good luck with that one, especially if you're asking her to dive back into Dean's."

"It's not about that," Tyde snapped.

"Then what is it?" Lenny asked, though he really didn't care.

Tyde examined the man before him. Lenny was guilty of countless deaths. He had been responsible for so much of what happened over the last few days. He could have stopped the monsters or at least warned people. He was a terrible person, which was why Tyde felt compelled to spill the skeletons from his closet and scatter their dusty bones before Lenny. He was just as bad, maybe worse and in no position to judge Tyde for his sins.

"Wendy had an affair a few years ago with one our friends, Tim," Tyde said. "Tim was always kind of a dick, but that never bothered me too much. We were really only friends because the three of us used to dive together all the time. Who cares if you're an ass if that's all it's really about, right?"

"Well, you know humans aren't really suited for marriage," Lenny waved dismissively. "Few animals are programmed for monogamy. I still don't see where her anger would come from, but then again, I never really understood marriage, love or any other made up silliness."

"She's not mad about the affair," Tyde continued. "I was mad about it. She's mad about what happened the last time the three of us went diving."

"And that would be?" Lenny asked. He didn't care about the stains splotched across some tourists' love life, but having them angry and upset might prove beneficial.

"We were doing a cave dive," Tyde added. "They thought I didn't know, but I did. I had suspected for a while and then caught them, but they never saw me, never knew what I saw. It killed me, just ate at me until all I could see was Tim and my wife…you need to understand how much I love her."

"Of course," Lenny nodded, pretending to have even the slightest notion of what Tyde called 'love.'

"We were almost done with the dive. Wendy swam ahead of us," Tyde said. "She wanted to explore an offshoot that was a little closer to the surface. I motioned to Tim because I had dropped my camera somewhere back in the cave. I left it there. He swam back with me to find it. When he went to grab the camera, I swam up behind him and pulled his regulator free. I just wanted to scare him, to let him know to stop messing around with my wife. He panicked, tried to attack me. I pushed him into one of walls, maybe too hard. I don't know. There were bubbles everywhere. When I got to the surface, I asked Wendy where Tim was, told her that he swam ahead of me because his air was low. She freaked out, started crying and screaming, so I went back under to find. I knew where he was."

Tyde toed a small pile of sand, recoiling when a tattered chunk of meat rolled out from underneath. "She never wanted to go diving again after the 'accident,' but I convinced her to come here to dive Dean's. We had always wanted to. It was going to save our marriage."

"See," Lenny nodded. "Now that I can understand. Humans, like most animals may not be programmed for marriage, but murder on the other hand, well we excel at that like no other. You shouldn't be ashamed for doing what nature has created you to do."

Lenny patted Tyde on the shoulder as he walked past him towards the water. He would never judge this man or ask him to explain his actions because Lenny certainly had no intentions of justifying what he was about to do.

-53-

Cal could hear the crabs in the distance. He waited in the front of the station, ensuring that the route was clear while Travis and Milo finished searching the station for anything of use. They scavenged two shotguns, an Uzi and a couple of handguns, but nothing like the rocket launcher Cal had hoped for. They had plenty of rounds; plenty of rounds and nothing that would stop a dinosaur, sea monster or whatever the hell waited for them in the water.

"Let's go," Travis slipped past Cal and walked towards a patrol car in the lot.

"Did you find keys to a boat?" Cal asked. He nervously swung a shotgun across the parking lot. Guns were never something he was comfortable with and his experience hitting a target was limited to video games, which was exactly why Travis had passed him a shotgun with the directions, 'pump, point and pull.' Cal thought about making a dirty joke, but somehow he got the feeling no one was in the mood.

"Right here," Milo said, twirling a ring of keys around his index finger. "This is to one of the large speed boats. I think it was something for chasing smugglers or drug runners or something. I figured it was our best bet." A large black duffle bag was thrown over his left shoulder.

"Too bad there isn't a plane or something," Cal groaned.

"Not too many of those around here and I'm sure if someone had one, that they've already left," Milo said. "Besides, there's no reason to waste time wishing on some shit that isn't going to happen."

"I guess," Cal muttered and trailed behind Milo as they made their way to patrol car. Travis was in the front seat with the engine running.

A click and then a thud shook the pavement behind Milo and Cal. A massive crab, its shell covered with clusters of jagged blue spikes, leapt from the roof. Claws flexed and clashed. Two beady black eyes caught the dying glow of the broken streetlights that tilted dangerously towards the street. They didn't need to turn around to know that they needed to run.

The crab scuttled forward on thin legs with a speed that seemed to defy its massive body. Cal swung the shotgun and fired wildly, tearing chunks of macadam free from the lot and scattering them uselessly under the advancing creature.

Travis steadied his arms on the roof of the patrol car and fired. His shots hit, momentarily stunning the crab, but doing little to cause it actual harm.

"Get back in the damn car," Milo shouted as he and Cal sprinted forward.

Cal could feel the claws closing around his stomach, slicing his flesh and crushing bones. He could feel death's icy fingers on the back of his neck. Oddly enough, all Cal could hear was thunder. The sky in front of him looked clear, stars shone, oblivious or uncaring of the violence that raged beneath them.

A second thunderclap sounded. The crab stumbled, one leg hung uselessly from a tattered thread of meat. The other legs scrambled to right the crab's tank-like body. It scuttled forward before a third bang stopped its progress.

The captain stood in the doorway of the station, a shotgun smoking in his hands.

Cal stared, unsure of what to do.

"Run, you moron." Milo grabbed Cal's arm and pulled him towards the patrol car.

The crab hesitated, deciding where the easier meal could be found. It turned and stumbled back towards the station, towards the captain.

The shotgun released a hollow *chunk* as the final shell was ejected. The captain turned the gun and swung the stock like a baseball bat. The swing went wide, spinning the captain.

Claws closed in from both sides, pinching together around his legs and ribs. Screams echoed over the dull crunch of bone. The captain refused to scream, his cowardice having run dry.

"We need to help him," Cal said, looking over his shoulder.

"He was helping us," Milo answered. "That kind of decision is one sided. There is no helping him. Let's go."

-54-

Beams of light sliced through the inky interior of the chamber leading down into Dean's Blue Hole. In magazines and online, it looked magical, like something from another planet. Painted in shades of blue and filled with creatures that existed nowhere else on Earth. The magic had disappeared, having been replaced with something heavy, something awful and not of this world or time. Now it just terrified Wendy.

Darkness leaked from behind the craggy outcroppings, like blood from between the teeth of a predator. Wendy tried to force the image from her mind. Her breathing became rapid and panicked. Mercurial bubbles streamed from the strange respirator in her mouth. Something tugged her arm and Wendy had to fight the urge to scream, to suck in a mouthful of water. To die.

Tim's cadaverous fingers, trailing bits of stringy flesh, bone exposed from the picking of small fish, wrapped around Wendy's arm. The waxen digits pulled at Wendy's soft flesh, found purchase and dug deeper. Tried to drag her down. Take her to some dark corner of the cave and tug the respirator from her mouth. Tim wanted her to understand what Tyde had done, wanted her to know firsthand. He wanted the same for her. Wendy squeezed her eyes

Tyde held her by the elbow. His eyes were shot with concern. He motioned with his hand. A simple thumbs up. The motion asked countless questions, spoke volumes.

Wendy nodded.

What was there to say? Was she okay? Far from it, but saying otherwise served no purpose. This was no longer about being okay or saving a marriage. It was only about surviving. Everything else could wait.

Tyde let go of Wendy's arm. He waited for her to begin swimming again, to follow Lenny deeper into Dean's. Their plan, if it could really be called that, was to set charges in the deeper sections of the cave. Once they were clear they would detonate the explosives, hopefully killing the creature or at the very least, trapping it.

Lenny seemed convinced that the plan would work. Tyde was unsure. How could they hope to trap something that had shattered the fetters of time? The heavy bag strapped to the strange doctor's side provided no solace.

The floor of Dean's came into view. Clouds of sandy bloomed with each flippered kick, rising like specters from unmarked graves. Lenny spun in the water, turning to this side and dropping the heavy bag to the seafloor.

Wendy and Tyde stared gentle motion of the water pulled at the flap of the bag, revealing its contents.

Rocks.

The bag was stuffed with rocks. There were no explosives.

Swim! Swim now! Tyde willed the thought to Wendy. They needed to get away from Lenny. They were stupid to trust him in the first place.

A shadow passed overhead like a low flying jet. Tyde and Wendy stopped. The shadow turned in a slow circled and began its decent.

Something silver flashed and passed through the water. Tyde momentarily thought a school of fish was fleeing the creature. His leg stung, salt burning a fresh wound. Thin tendrils of red wound through the water, drifting upwards, calling to the monster. They were trapped.

The narrow opening leading to rocky ledge beckoned, signaling a small glimmer of hope. Jefferson led them there on the previous dive and it cost him his life. Now it was the only hope to save theirs.

-55-

Returning to the marina was one of the last things that Milo wanted to do, ranking only marginally above staying on the island and waiting to get eaten by a giant crab.

"Where are the RBDF boats docked?" Travis asked as he pulled the patrol car behind a large dumpster and turned off the engine. The marina parking lot was quiet. Somewhere on the other side of the property the seawall slipped into the water, a makeshift grave for Milo's brother. Seeing people die was nothing new to Travis. Hell, during his last detail in Roswell, New Mexico, he had seen an entire town devoured by an obese teenager, his body infested with a sentient alien slime. But this one caught him off guard.

Stan was a good man; perhaps one of the few remaining on this planet and Travis could see that he loved his brother. He could also see that Milo and Stan's relationship had never been an easy one. They had probably spent most of their time beating the crap out of each other, but that did little to lessen the pain. Travis only hoped that Stan had drowned and not been eaten by that monster. Sadly, that was what passed for hope.

"There," Milo pointed towards a long shadow on the far side of the parking lot.

"What about one of the larger ones?" Cal asked. He pointed towards two massive ships.

"The smaller ones are better," Milo said. "We aren't going to get very far in one of those. They max out around thirty miles per hour."

Cal scoffed, "In case you haven't noticed, that dinosaur is fucking huge. I'd feel much better in a bigger boat with guns on it."

"Enough," Travis cut in. "We're taking the speed boat. Let's just get going."

The water was dark and glassy. Streaks of red and pink cut across the sky as the sun struggled to pull itself above the horizon.

Everyone hesitated on the dock, though none wanted to admit it.

"I'll drive," Milo said. He climbed down into the boat. "Get the lines and be ready to jump. As soon as the engine starts up that thing is going come looking, so we need to move."

Cal and Travis tugged at the thick lines that tied the boat to the dock.

"We're good," Travis said.

Milo twisted the key and twin engines roared to life, sputtered and died. A cloud of black smoke drifted from the engines.

"Should we try a different boat?" Cal asked.

Something moved in the deeper waters, not far from the end of the dock. It could have been the tide or a passing school of fish.

"No time." Milo turned the key again. The engines chugged, belched smoke and roared to life. "Good enough. Let's go."

The other men leapt from the dock, landing in the waiting boat. Cal's feet shot out from under him, his head and feet trading places. There was a hollow *thunk* as Cal's head bounced off the deck of the boat. Cal groaned and tried to climb to his feet, but collapsed back onto the deck.

"Stay there," Travis said. "You're going to hurt yourself or shoot one of us." Cal nodded.

The boat chugged in reverse until Milo shifted and pulled the throttle back.

Cal heard a roar, thought it might be the engines struggling to meet the demands placed upon them by Milo.

"Get up," Travis demanded. "Get up right now."

"I thought you said to stay here," Cal groaned.

"Now," Travis shouted over the engines.

The engines growled in fits of mechanical rage, but something echoed above them. Something primal. Something alive.

A swell grew and pulsed, becoming a moving wall of water. Travis aimed the Uzi and fired. The bullets disappeared into the water, doing little to slow it down.

As the obsidian surface of the sea parted, an elongated snout, nearly as long as the boat took shape. A tangled nest of teeth jutted from the side, more revealed as the creature's head emerged from the water, an ancient call breaking free from its cavernous throat.

Cal steadied himself, his possible concussion suddenly less threatening. He lined up a shot.

"Just fucking fire already!" Milo shouted over his shoulder.

More rounds were absorbed by the water.

"It's gone," Travis said. "Where the hell did it go?"

"Who cares?" Cal asked. "It's gone. Isn't that enough?"

"It's a predator," Milo said. "The only way it would give up the hunt is if there was an easier meal."

"Easier meal?" Cal repeated.

"Get to Dean's," Travis barked over the engines. "Make this thing go faster."

-56-

The blood thinned, almost disappearing as it wafted higher on the gentle currents. It would be completely unseen to most. Not all.

The creature sensed the blood, the invisible tendrils twisting through the water and stirring its most basic, yet strongest need. To hunt. To feed. This was the creature's purpose, what it had been created to do.

Broad, oar-like, flippers pushed the creature deeper into the cave, closer to its prey, to the source of the blood. These waters were filled with food, some easier to catch than others, but the creature did not know how to become discouraged. When one prey became difficult, another would become available.

Three waited below.

Tyde followed Wendy into the narrow offshoot that led to the rocky ledge. Lenny was somewhere behind them, but after he slashed Tyde's leg he had seemingly disappeared. Bubbles trailed behind Wendy, more than usual. Her breathing was frantic. Tyde had limited knowledge of the experimental diving gear, but panicked breathing would deplete any supply.

The walls of the passage shook as the monster rammed its gnarled snout into the sides. Teeth gnashed, crushing the rocks caught between powerful jaws.

The ledge loomed overhead. Wendy's feet disappeared over the side as she pulled herself out of the water. Tyde followed.

"You're bleeding," Wendy said, her words thin and forced. Her shoulders heaved as she struggled to breath.

"I'm fine," Tyde said without looking. The truth was that he had no idea how deep Lenny had cut him. Investigating the wound would only serve to further upset the both of them. Tyde pulled a knife from the sheath on his ankle. Blood coated his arm. He sliced a long strip from the left leg of his bathing suit, wrapped it around the gash and tightly knotted it. Blood welled around the makeshift bandage.

"You're not," Wendy said. Her breathing had slowed.

Tyde laughed dryly. "No, I guess I'm not."

"Neither of us are," Wendy added. "We never were."

"Is this really the time?" Tyde snapped. "There's a fucking dinosaur waiting out there to eat us and you want to have an impromptu couple's therapy session? Seriously?"

"You know you're a real asshole," Wendy snapped.

"I'm an asshole?" Tyde asked. "Yeah, maybe. But at least I never cheated on you."

"No, you just murdered someone," Wendy said. "Let me bask in the holy glow of Saint Tyde. Oh please, let me model my life in your pious image, you sanctimonious asshole."

"I didn't murder him," Tyde said.

"Call it whatever you need to." Wendy turned her back and hugged her knees to her chest.

"I fought with Tim, wanted to scare him," Tyde said. "I just wanted him to...to stop what he was doing. What you were both doing. I just wanted him to go away so we could have time to fix our marriage. I just wanted time. I never wanted what happened to him."

"Time?" Wendy spat. "That's all you keep talking about. Time. Jeez, Tyde, all we've ever had is time and all we've ever done with it is use it to further fuck up the other one. How can we fix a marriage that's fucking toxic?"

"It wasn't always," Tyde protested weakly.

"No, I guess not," Wendy answered. "But really, was it ever a marriage? We had fun together and thought that getting married would keep that going, but it didn't. It killed it. It's going to kill both of us too."

"I married you because I love you," Tyde said. "Not because it was fun. It was never fun."

"Exactly," Wendy nodded. "But what good is loving each other if that's what it does to us? We never should have gotten married. It never should have gone beyond a vacation fling."

"Yeah, well it's a little late for that," Tyde said. "How much air do you have left?"

"Change of subject?" Wendy laughed, though devoid of humor. "Not much."

"Take my tanks." Tyde pushed them towards his wife. "Keep your breathing controlled."

"We're going back in the water? With that thing? And that insane doctor?" Wendy shook her head. "No, I'm not going."

"Staying here isn't much of an option," Tyde said. "Besides, I'm sure you'd prefer different company."

"Tyde," Wendy began. "I didn't mean to–"

"It doesn't matter," Tyde cut in. "Not any more. Just get the tanks on and stay behind me."

-57-

A narrow channel led into Dean's Blue Hole. Milo had guided his boat through countless times, but never with the trepidation that he currently felt. The water was calm and dark, a few small swells undulated across the surface. There was no sign of the monster, but the ocean could hide anything, even a prehistoric nightmare.

"Do you see anyone?" Milo shouted to Travis, who stood in the bow of the boat, his Uzi trained on the water. The engines rumbled as Milo shifted into neutral; he thought about turning them off, hoping to avoid the attention of the monster, but didn't relish the idea of trying to restart the engines if it appeared.

"It'll know we're here either way," Cal said, as if aware of Milo's concerns. "Let the engines idle, I get the feeling we might need to get out of here soon."

"There," Travis motioned towards a small shadowy form in the water.

Milo turned the steering wheel and let the boat glide towards the shape.

"I'm so glad to see you," Lenny waved from the water. He belched and silvery stream of liquid oxygen splashed into the water. "Get me out of here."

"Where are Tyde and Wendy?" Travis asked. His words were sharp and punctuated with the barrel of his gun.

"The creature got them," Lenny lied. "We dove into Dean's to set off explosives and hopefully trap the monster, but we weren't successful. Now get me out of here before it comes back. We need to leave now."

"How'd you get away?" Cal questioned.

"All these pointless questions can be answered in the damn boat. Now get me out of the water," Lenny demanded.

"Just get him," Milo said.

"But he used people as bait before," Cal protested. "He'd do it again. I say we leave him."

"I can't say that I entirely disagree," Travis added. "If Tyde and Wendy are missing, then it's a safe bet that this asshole had something to do with it. Leave him."

"What about Tyde and Wendy?" Cal asked.

"We'll do a lap," Milo said. "Make sure they're not on the shore or in the water. Then we need to go."

"Wonderful plan," Lenny chimed in. "Now if you'd be so kind." He held his arms up.

Cal moved to the back of the boat where a small platform and water waited. He held out his hand as Lenny swam around the side of the boat. "Over here."

"There!" Travis pointed to a spot a few hundred feet off the bow of the boat.

Something moved in the water, at first no more than a few ripples, but growing in size and rising like a small island.

There was hardly enough room for the monster to turn its sleek body and head towards the rumbling echo of the approaching boat engines. Tyde was relieved to see the monster turn away from hunting him and Wendy, but knew that what had drawn it away was probably Milo and the others. This was a temporary reprieve at best and most likely a death sentence.

Turning back to Wendy, Tyde motioned towards the surface. She nodded and waited for him to swim out into the main chamber of Dean's. Tyde kept close to the wall. He had no idea how the creature hunted, sight, smell, some primitive ability to detect electrical impulses in the water – any were plausible. Still, staying out of sight seemed like a good idea no matter the mechanism by which the monster hunted.

Slipping over the edge of Dean's and into open water felt like a hollow victory. In the distance, Tyde could hear the mechanical growl of the a boat engine, but being underwater, had no real way of determining its direction. A strange chopping sound joined the roar of the boat engines revving up.

Wendy frantically motioned towards the surface. Tyde knew what worried her, sharing the same concern of being left behind. They could stay underwater and risk missing their only chance to be rescued or break the surface and risk being eaten. The promise of temporary safety could not be allowed to outweigh the possibility of an actual escape.

Bullets peppered the surface of the water, throwing small sprays of water into the air surrounding the monster. Tyde couldn't help but picture a hellish fountain showcasing the nightmarish relic from a time man was never intended to know.

A sleek, gray speedboat cut a tight circle around the monster while people onboard fired at the creature. The monster bellowed, equal parts anger and pain, as it attempted and failed to catch the boat.

"They can't do that forever," Wendy said, treading water next Tyde. She opened her mouth to say more, but a thick liquid gushed forward, splattering into the surrounding water. A second stream of the experimental oxygen spilled from Tyde's mouth. It was cold, driving a chill through his bones and twisting his guts.

"Your tank is empty," Wendy coughed. The needle of the gauge on Tyde's shoulder strap had dropped solidly into the red. He must have been without air for the majority of their swim for the surface, but never once panicked or tried to buddy breath. Tyde had wanted to keep her calm, keep her safe. He always had. Wendy found herself regretting so much.

"So is my stomach," Tyde replied.

The monster dropped beneath the water, leaving only salty spray and turbulent water in its wake.

"Over here!" Tyde began swimming towards the boat.

"They won't hear us over the engines," Wendy said.

Tyde stopped swimming. Wendy was right, but was there really a need to be nihilistic when the odds were already stacked against them. Tyde wanted to say something cutting, to hurt Wendy like she had hurt him, but he kept his mouth closed.

Pulling a small orange cylinder from his shoulder, Tyde pushed the gray rubber button and hurled it towards the boat. The strobe began flashing.

"Turn yours on too," Tyde said. Wendy did.

The first strobe disappeared into a yawning whirlpool as the creature's massive jaws emerged and snapped shut.

"Turn it off Wendy," Tyde said. "Turn it off."

"I can't." Wendy fumbled with the strobe light. "It won't turn off. I can't turn it off."

Water swelled as the monster was drawn to the flashing light and clicking sound it emitted.

"Give me the strobe." Tyde held out his hand. "Wendy, give it to me."

She hesitated. Tyde snatched the flashing light from her dive harness.

"Tyde!" Wendy protested as he swam away.

Somewhere in the distance, Tyde could hear the roar of the boat engine drowning out the cries of his wife.

-59-

Milo watched as Tyde began swimming across Dean's. The water swelled and pulsed around him, but the creature had yet to appear. It wouldn't be long before both the tourist and flashing strobe disappeared.

The boat engines revved as Milo swung it towards Tyde.

"What are you doing, you idiot?" Lenny belched from the passenger seat bolted to the deck of the boat. Milo cast a dirty look as Lenny released a torrent of mercurial liquid into the boat. "He's drawing it away so she can escape. Go get her." The doctor sat awkwardly in the seat, his dive gear still strapped to his back, a boxy black bag hung from its belt. Out of habit, Cal had moved to help Lenny out of the rig, but thought better of it and left his former employer as he was when they pulled him from the water.

Milo's hand drifted to the handgun tucked into the waistband of his board shorts. Shooting Lenny seemed like a pretty reasonable decision given that Milo was convinced that he had used Tyde and Wendy as bait. Now Tyde was doing the same thing, but for completely different reasons.

"She's over there," Travis shouted from the bow of the boat.

Cal frantically swept the barrel of his shotgun back and forth across the surface of the water. "Where? Where?"

"Put that shit down before you shoot her," Travis snapped and pushed the barrel of the gun down.

Wendy held her arms overhead, hands clasped, the universal dive signal that she was okay. Okay was a bit of a stretch given the circumstance, but Travis figured there were a limited number of motions one could do while treading water.

"Slow down," Cal shouted. Milo pushed the throttle towards neutral and let the boat glide forward.

Hanging over the side of the boat, Cal and Travis hauled Wendy out of the water and into the boat. She splashed across the seats lining the bow and thudded onto the deck.

"Are you okay?" Cal asked, not knowing a better question.

"Tyde," Wendy gasped. "Get Tyde."

Cal helped Wendy to her feet and balanced her as she walked towards the back of the boat. Her tanks were cumbersome, but somehow she managed to get back to Milo and Lenny without falling.

The flashing of the strobe ceased. The water was dark and quiet. Something splashed, but Milo couldn't be sure if it was a fish, the monster or Tyde.

"Leave him," Lenny demanded. "He knew what he was doing and why he was doing it. It sure as hell wasn't for us to wait around and get eaten next."

"Shut your mouth," Milo snapped.

"I'm just saying that his sacrifice shouldn't be in vain," Lenny argued. "That's all."

"Next word out of your mouth will be followed by a bullet from my gun," Milo leveled the barrel of his handgun with Lenny's face.

"He didn't sacrifice anything," Wendy added. "He's alive. He's going to be fine." Lenny thought about the idiocy of her words, opened his mouth to argue, but thought better of it once he looked at Milo's gun.

"Over there." Travis pointed somewhere to the left. Milo couldn't see anything. No Tyde. No strobe. No monster.

"Where?" Milo yelled back.

But the question answered itself as the water parted like velvet stage curtains to reveal the creature's sleek head. With the day slowly chasing away the night, it was difficult to make out a great deal of detail. The large, crocodilian skull was more than enough to inspire Milo to swing the steering wheel hard to the right and gun the engines.

There was a loud gurgle, a mechanical chug and black smoke.

"The engines just quit," Milo groaned. "Again."

"I am relieved to see that I am not the only genius on the boat," Lenny smiled, completely devoid of humor.

"Start helping or shut up." Travis pushed past Lenny.

"I thought I was," Lenny said.

Travis thought about passing a weapon to Wendy or Lenny. She could hardly stand and he was more likely to turn it on someone inside the boat. "Looks like it's us," Travis said to Cal. "Remember the drill?"

"Point, pull and pump," Cal repeated.

"Just like your teenage years," Travis grinned. A little gallows humor never hurt.

Milo moved to the rear of the boat and pulled the covers off the smoking twin engines. Greasy tendrils of smoke wafted around his head, becoming tangled in his dreadlocks. Thick, black liquid leaked across the guts of the engine.

"Is it bad?" Cal asked. He watched the creature move closer. It swam with ease, an almost instinctual confidence. It may have never encountered boats or mankind before, but the predatory folds of its brain knew lame prey when it saw it.

"Yeah," Milo said. "But focus on the water. Try to buy me some time."

"Give me a gun," Lenny demanded.

"I'll give you a bullet," Travis said. "Now get over to the controls and be ready to start the engines when Milo tells you to."

"Certainly, Ms. Daisy," Lenny said. He collapsed into the other seat and waited for the go ahead to get the hell out of here – something he had been advocating for since they pulled him into the boat. Wasting time trying to save people only got other people killed. It was simple math – with Lenny being greater than all other variables.

The creature surged beneath the water, a swell colliding with the side of the boat. Travis stumbled and fell on top of Cal, who hit the deck of the boat with a hollow *thud*. Lenny slipped from the driver's seat, flailing and trying to regain his balance by lurching for the steering wheel. The engines swung with the wheel as Lenny fell, knocking Milo into the water. The heavy tanks on Lenny's back carried him out of the seat and into Wendy. The added weight of her air tanks swept the two of them over the side of the boat.

Water flooded Wendy's mouth and nostrils. She tried not to suck in more, but her lungs demanded air. She clawed at the water, trying to pull herself past Lenny. Weight belts and air tanks tugged them downwards, towards the bottom, closer to death. Somewhere beneath or beside them, the creature waited. It swam and hunted.

***

Tyde swam. There was nothing left to do. It seemed simple and on most days it would have been. Concern for Wendy, for the others, for himself, clawed at this chest and twisted his heart. Tyde's panicked breaths rippled the water as he continued to slap the surface and pull himself forward. Tyde could have swam with more grace, could have dropped his tanks and made faster progress, but he needed to attract the monster, to draw it away from the others.

The surface of the water behind Tyde was still, a darkened sheet of glass. No monster, at least not on the surface.

Tyde looked towards the shore, his mind screaming that he get out of the water, that he find safety. There was none to be found.

Dark shapes, hunched and spiny, scuttled across the beach. Claws clashed as the monstrous crabs scurried along the shoreline, hesitant to enter the water where the other creature waited, but anxious for a meal.

"Where the hell are you?" Tyde asked. He did not want to see it, wanted to get eaten even less, but he couldn't let the others die.

There were a series of splashes. A few startled shouts. Something happened to the boat, to everyone on it. He started swimming towards the boat.

Tyde had failed again.

***

Something passed beneath Wendy. She felt the pull of sand papery skin slide across her flesh. A metallic screech echoed through the water. The dive rig on Wendy's back lurched backwards. The salt water stung Wendy's eyes, but she forced them open. The blurry image of Lenny's body shot past her.

The straps on her tanks jerked again. Wendy gasped, cold water gushed, burning like acid and filling her lungs. Black began to leak into the edges of Wendy's vision. Her head throbbed. Her fingers fumbled with the straps on her dive rig, weakly pulling at the buckles. The straps remained in place.

The creature's jaws closed around the air tanks as it dove deeper, pulling Lenny and Wendy further beneath the water.

***

Milo broke the surface of the water. He could feel the sting of salt water in the gash on his forehead from where the engine's prop tore his flesh. The blood would call to the monster. In the deeper reaches of Milo's mind, a dinner bell chimed.

"Give me your hand," Travis said. He looked worn, but was still inside the boat. Cal stood beside him. They pulled Milo from the water.

"Like landing a giant fish," Cal smirked.

"We've got enough of those around here already," Milo groaned. "Where are the others?"

"Wendy and Lenny never resurfaced." Travis tried to remain composed, to sound factual. Milo could hear the strain in Travis' words.

"Over here," a voice called. It was Tyde.

Moments later, Tyde was in the boat.

"Where's Wendy," Tyde asked. His eyes bore into the three men still in the boat. "Where?"

"She went over the side," Milo said.

"You didn't go after her?" Tyde ran to the edge of the boat and peered into the dark water. "You didn't even try?"

Tyde pulled the knife from its sheath. He turned to look at the others and dove back into the water.

"Well, what now?" Cal asked.

"Get the engines working," Travis said. "We need to be ready to go when Tyde gets back."

Both Milo and Cal noticed that Travis only mentioned Tyde, not Wendy. They chose to ignore prophetic slip of words and focus on the boat.

***

Lenny twisted and slipped one shoulder free from the straps. The other remained twisted and refused to come free. The tanks strapped to his back crunched and pinched as the creature's teeth pressed closer together. Wendy's motionless body hung limply next to him.

A hand closed around Lenny's wrist. He turned, fighting the urge to scream, seconds later loathing himself for allowing fear to win out over intelligence.

Tyde pulled himself across Lenny's body, a knife clutched in one hand. He began sawing the straps of Wendy's dive rig.

The image of the knife flashed through Lenny's mind. It was his only out. Lenny grabbed for the knife, twisting Tyde's wrist and trying to take the blade.

Tyde turned and thrust the knife.

Something burned in Lenny's side. He still wanted the blade, wanted his freedom. When Tyde turned back to the futile task to trying to free his, most likely already dead, wife, Lenny made one last attempt for the knife.

The straps securing Wendy to monster shredded, finally separating from the tanks. Her limp body slumped forward and drifted towards the surface.

Tyde grabbed for Wendy, but something pulled him back, loosening his grip on the knife. It spun slowly and disappeared into the murky depths. Tyde tugged and struggled to free himself from Lenny's grip. His lungs protested, deprived of air. Spots swam through his vision. Tyde could feel Lenny pawing at him, perhaps in anger or a final feeble plea for help.

The knife wound slowly wept blood. Tyde had no weapon, no weapon other than his own primal urges to survive. He turned towards Lenny and saw two things – a small black pouch on the doctor's belt and a large gash. With one hand, Tyde grabbed the pouch. With the other he thrust his fingers into the wound, grasping the soft flesh and pulling. He tugged and twisted the meat until something snapped and came loose.

Bubbles erupted from Lenny's mouth as he screamed. Tyde's attack freed Lenny's arm and the doctor floated into open water. Tyde wanted to follow Lenny, to continue to cause him pain, to kill him. He needed to follow Wendy. He needed air.

This pouch held small, tan bricks – explosives, not rocks. The ones Lenny should have left at the bottom of Dean's. Tyde wound the frayed straps of Wendy's rig around the pouch. A small black box was tucked inside. Tyde fumbled with the buttons.

The darkness took over. Tyde could no longer fight it.

***

A body bobbed motionlessly on the surface of the water. It was Wendy. Lenny and Tyde followed close behind.

"Try the engine," Milo said.

Cal twisted the key. The engines groaned as if in protest before coughing a cloud of black smoke and sputtering to life.

The throttle edged forward, Cal hesitant to gun the engines and attract the attention of the monster.

A muffled roar echoed, its ferocity softened by fathoms of water.

"What was th–" Milo's words were cut short as a pillar of water erupted from the center of Dean's, blossoming like a mushroom cloud. The boat dipped forward, riding into the trough created by the explosion.

"Hang on," Travis yelled.

The pillar dissolved into a frothy, tumbling storm, large waves radiating away from its center. The bow of the boat dipped beneath one wave, only to be slammed by the next, pulled deeper beneath the water.

There was no choice but to abandon ship. The boat was swamped. Travis leapt into the next wave, Milo and Cal close behind.

The three men swam for shore, each towing a body with them.

Travis made land first. The crabs were close, reluctantly edging around the small rise that led onto the beach. Travis pulled Wendy onto the beach. She wasn't moving. He fell to his knees and began rescue breathing. Nothing. More breaths. More desperate compressions. Still nothing.

Milo and Cal dragged Tyde and Lenny onto the beach. Both were awake.

"Wendy," Tyde coughed. "Where is she?"

"She's…" Travis stepped away, his legs coated with sand. "I'm sorry, Tyde."

"No, no, no, no," Tyde murmured as he crawled through the sand. How could she be gone? They had survived this long. Tyde cradled his wife and cried.

"She drowned," Travis said, not knowing what to say, but feeling unable to remain silent. "I tried. I'm sorry."

"What was that explosion?" Milo asked, eyeing the water. He turned towards Lenny.

"I'm bleeding," Lenny said from where he lay in the sand, the water gently licking his feet. "In case any of you cared."

"We don't," Cal said and kicked a small pile of sand towards his former employer. "Answer the question."

"Jeez, talk about priorities," Lenny groaned. "It was probably a combination of the liquid oxygen and explosives."

"Is it dead?" Cal asked.

"Do you see chunks of sea monster bobbing on the surface?" Lenny said. "Dead things tend to float, especially pieces of them."

"So what happened to it?" Milo asked.

"Who knows?" Lenny said. He pushed himself up to a sitting position, pain etched into his face. "An explosion of that magnitude could have collapsed the inner chamber of Dean's. Maybe it's dead. Or more likely it's just trapped."

"Good," Milo said. "Either way it's dead or dying."

"Not quite, my overly optimistic friend," Lenny cut in. "Dead? Maybe. Trapped? Certainly not. There are tunnels leading out of Dean's to a myriad of other locations. If that wondrous creature is still alive, the last thing it is, is trapped."

Travis walked over and knelt next to Tyde. "I know this is going to be hard, but we need to go. We can't stay here." The crabs inched closer, still aware of the sea monster, but emboldened by the close proximity of food.

"I can't leave her here," Tyde said, his voice barely above a whisper. "Go without me if you want."

"Not happening," Travis said and pulled Tyde up from the ground. Tyde lashed out, trying to strike Travis and collapsed back to the sand, his body trembling with choked sobs.

"Give him some time," Cal said.

"We don't have any." Travis motioned towards the rise as the first crab, either braver or hungrier than the others, scuttled forward.

Small plumes of sand leapt into the air, the tang of cordite wafting along lazy salt breezes from across the water.

The crab's legs buckled and twisted, its shell pocked and chipped from large caliber rounds. The others scuttled forward, eager to feast on an easy meal, even if it was one of their own.

A matte black helicopter hovered silently over the water, its blades causing the surface to ripple and dance.

"I thought stealth helicopters were only a myth," Cal said, staring at the craft. "Like something that seemed like a good idea, but never really worked."

"That's what the government wants you to think," Travis said. He waved his arms towards the sleek helicopter. It turned and headed towards shore.

The helicopter touched down in a swirling sandstorm. The crabs were busy eating, but it wouldn't last long.

"Agent Howard, sir," a soldier clad completely in black stepped out of the helicopter, pushing up the visor on his helmet. "Sir, we need to go. We are expected to report to the Peach Island facility by zero five hundred tomorrow, sir"

"Help me load this woman on board," Travis said.

"Negative, sir," the soldier answered. "We have weight restrictions and my orders are to retrieve you and Dr. Borges, sir."

"How much can we carry?" Travis asked as he walked towards the soldier.

"My apologies sir, but I don't think I made myself clear," the soldier said. "My orders only detailed the recovery of you and Dr. Borges, sir. Weight restrictions are less of an issue than my orders, sir."

Before the soldier knew what happened, Travis snatched the pistol from where it was strapped to the other man's leg.

"Sir?"

Travis spun and fired one round. Lenny's body went limp, the sand slowly turning black.

"Load her."

***

Sand swept across the beach, caught up in the artificial dust devils created by the helicopter's rotors.

Lenny coughed, blood spattering his lips. A cloying metallic taste crept through his mouth. It was bad, Lenny knew that much. Sand clung to the blood on Lenny's face.

It hurt to move, to breath, but Lenny pushed himself up to a sitting position. The morning sun forced its way higher into the silken sky. A few stars clung to the vanishing darkness, the light a beacon that called to Lenny for reasons he did not understand. Nature. Beauty. These were things that Lenny never had the time; let alone the interest to ponder. But now, bleeding on this beach, Lenny found himself entranced by the dying flicker of these lights. The scientific part of Lenny's mind knew that by the time these lights reached Earth that their source was most likely dead. Their decayed beauty an unwavering source of artistic inspiration and fascination for eons of humans, now were Lenny's only source of comfort.

A dry scratching sound rustled behind Lenny. He knew what was coming, knew there could be only one outcome – where the bullet had failed, the crabs would surely succeed.

The water covering Dean's rippled and shifted. A large curved form broke the surface, calling to mind old Loch Ness hoax photos, or at least what most assumed were hoaxes. Its massive head lifted from the water, perhaps checking for danger or food, before disappearing. The angle of the creature's body led Lenny to believe that it dove down, back into Dean's, into the tunnels – tunnels that could take it across the globe.

Lenny could not help but smile. The creature, his creature, had survived. He knew that it would. There had never been a doubt. Dinosaur, monster or myth, it did not really matter. This glorious creature had survived the relentless march of time, had proven to Lenny that there were still dark corners of the world waiting to be illuminated by science. Now it was free to find another corner where it could hide, could hunt.

Something scuttled across the sand, this time much closer. Lenny kept his eyes on the water, silently urging the creature onward.

The soft flesh of Lenny's belly puckered and peeled back like the petals of a revolting blossom. Blood spilled across his lap in thick waves of unsettling warmth. The javelin-like leg of the crab pushed further through Lenny's body, splintering bone and erupting from his back. Lenny coughed and tried to remain sitting, pawing at the spire that speared him to the ground. He tried to keep his eyes on the water, hopeful to see another glimpse of the creature, as the crab's claws separated his head from the rest of his body.

Author's Note

Agent Travis Howard first appeared in *Pink Slime* published by Severed Press. If you want to know his back-story or why he will never eat Jell-O give *Pink Slime* a read.

CHECK OUT OTHER GREAT DEEP SEA THRILLERS

MEGA
by Jake Bible

There is something in the deep. Something large. Something hungry. Something prehistoric.
And Team Grendel must find it, fight it, and kill it.
Kinsey Thorne, the first female US Navy SEAL candidate has hit rock bottom. Having washed out of the Navy, she turned to every drink and drug she could get her hands on. Until her father and cousins, all ex-Navy SEALS themselves, offer her a way back into the life: as part of a private, elite combat Team being put together to find and hunt down an impossible monster in the Indian Ocean. Kinsey has a second chance, but can she live through it?

THE BLACK
by Paul E Cooley

Under 30,000 feet of water, the exploration rig Leaguer has discovered an oil field larger than Saudi Arabia, with oil so sweet and pure, nations would go to war for the rights to it. But as the team starts drilling exploration well after exploration well in their race to claim the sweet crude, a deep rumbling beneath the ocean floor shakes them all to their core. Something has been living in the oil and it's about to give birth to the greatest threat humanity has ever seen.

"The Black" is a techno/horror-thriller that puts the horror and action of movies such as Leviathan and The Thing right into readers' hands. Ocean exploration will never be the same."

CHECK OUT OTHER GREAT
DEEP SEA THRILLERS

PREDATOR X
by C.J Waller

When deep level oil fracking uncovers a vast subterranean sea, a crack team of cavers and scientists are sent down to investigate. Upon their arrival, they disappear without a trace. A second team, including sedimentologist Dr Megan Stoker, are ordered to seek out Alpha Team and report back their findings. But Alpha team are nowhere to be found – instead, they are faced with something unexpected in the depths. Something ancient. Something huge. Something dangerous. Predator X

DEAD BAIT
by Tim Curran

A husband hell-bent on revenge hunts a Wereshark...A Russian mail order bride with a fishy secret...Crabs with a collective consciousness...A vampire who transforms into a Candiru...Zombie piranha...Bait that will have you crawling out of your skin and more. Drawing on horror, humor with a helping of dark fantasy and a touch of deviance, these 19 contemporary stories pay homage to the monsters that lurk in the murky waters of our imaginations. If you thought it was safe to go back in the water...Think Again!

CHECK OUT OTHER GREAT DEEP SEA THRILLERS

LAMPREYS
by Alan Spencer

A secret government tactical team is sent to perform a clean sweep of a private research installation. Horrible atrocities lurk within the abandoned corridors. Mutated sea creatures with insane killing abilities are waiting to suck the blood and meat from their prey.

Unemployed college professor Conrad Garfield is forced to assist and is soon separated from the team. Alone and afraid, Conrad must use his wits to battle mutated lampreys, infected scientists and go head-to-head with the biggest monstrosity of all.

Can Conrad survive, or will the deadly monsters suck the very life from his body?

DEEP DEVOTION
by M.C. Norris

Rising from the depths, a mind-bending monster unleashes a wave of terror across the American heartland. Kate Browning, a Kansas City EMT confronts her paralyzing fear of water when she traces the source of a deadly parasitic affliction to the Gulf of Mexico. Cooperating with a marine biologist, she travels to Florida in an effort to save the life of one very special patient, but the source of the epidemic happens to be the nest of a terrifying monster, one that last rose from the depths to annihilate the lost continent of Atlantis.

Leviathan, destroyer, devoted lifemate and parent, the abomination is not going to take the extermination of its brood well.